By Your Leave

BY: KAREN PIVOTT

www.amazon.com/author/karenpivott

BY THE SAME AUTHOR
BOOKS ON KINDLE and IN PRINT
NON FICTION
Airbags and Starting Over
Back On the Road Again
Always Travel With Your Basket
CHILDRENS FICTION
Birthdays at the Bay
Royce and Billy
FICTION
By Any Other Circumstances
By Any And All Means
By Your Leave

FOREWORD

Jenna a woman now well into her middle years has not only learned many of life's lessons, she has also learned the value of them, and it is the values that Jenna has learned over time that enables her to confront her past fully, be true to herself and find enduring freedom in the rewards life presents her with, as interesting people join her along the way. Some of those people move on, while others continue to add colour and flavor to Jenna's own life and experiences.......

BY YOUR LEAVE

Disclaimer
This is a work of fiction.   Names, characters,
businesses, places, events and incidents are either
the product of the author's imagination or used in
a fictitious manner.   Any resemblance to actual
persons, living or dead, or actual events is purely
coincidental

CONTENTS

Acknowledgement

With thanks and love always to my husband
Alan.

KAREN PIVOTT

CHAPTER ONE

Jenna had enjoyed a wonderful break away. It had been two years since she had seen her family and she had relished the time she had spent with them. Unlike her previous homecoming there were no notices about earthworks commencing with dust warnings. No this return home was very uneventful.

Jenna had phoned her neighbour Anne Brown to let her know she was back, and they agreed to meet up the following morning at ten o'clock. Jenna was pleased about this and began putting clothes into the washing machine that needed attention. Turning the machine on, she then went to her bedroom and began putting her other clothes away.

Getting the shuttle to and from the airport had been a great way to go, and Jenna decided she would do that again, if she was fortunate enough to go again.

Jenna's thoughts were interrupted by the phone ringing. Not home even an hour she thought as picked the handset up "Hello Jenna? It's Jean. Just phoning to make sure you are home safe and sound. I won't hold you up."

"Yes Jean I am, and thank you."

"Good trip was it? The family well?"

"Yes I've had a lovely time with them all. Jean I am just in the process of unpacking before I go into town to get some bits and pieces."

"Yes. We will talk soon. Glad you're back." Jean said ending the call.

Jenna went into the kitchen filled the jug, and got one of the herbal tea bags from her jar on the kitchen shelf. She located a large cup from the cupboard and put the tea bag into it. Returning to the bedroom she put the last of her things away and took out a wrapped gift at the

bottom of her bag. Opening the wrapping
gently and placing the item on the bed
Jenna smiled as she remembered choosing
this from the gift store with Vincent and
Brittany in tow. The gift voucher covered
a good part of the purchase price and
Jenna gladly paid the difference. "Now
where am I going to put you?" she asked
out loud and followed that with "Just as
helpful as the Hat I see." Walking with the
oil painting an autumn scene of the region
where Vincent and Brittany lived, Jenna
found a place in her formal living room
where the light was perfect for it, and
where it wouldn't get too much light for
too long during the day. Placing the
picture on her sofa Jenna went to the
garage to get the picture hooks and a
hammer and returned via the kitchen
where she put the boiled water into her
mug. While her tea drew she made her
way to the living room where she promptly
hammered in the picture hook and placed
the picture upon it. Standing back she
checked for straightness, made a slight
adjustment, before returning her hammer
to the garage.

On her way back through to the
kitchen to get her cup of tea Jenna

stopped and put her suitcase away. Walking along the hallway she spoke to the Hat "I hope you are happy. I have the washing on and everything put away, and now I will have my tea before hanging the washing out and making my way into town to get some groceries and a bit of dinner. Any suggestions? Of course not." Jenna said. Sitting with her cup of tea in her favourite chair next to the window in her lounge Jenna felt quite pleased with herself. A lie in the following morning would be very welcome. I will set my alarm for nine o'clock so I get to Anne's on time.

In no time at all Jenna had finished her cup of tea and was hanging her washing on the line. How lucky she thought to have a covered area where I can hang my washing out to get the sun and the wind but miss the rain. The covered area had originally been for a trailer and was located just at the rear of the house. Jenna had used it spasmodically for a place to sit when she had her drinks outside or when she was gardening. The space was perfect for putting tools down or plants onto the table Jenna had placed there with a couple of chairs. It was Dorothy her neighbour two doors along who had suggested she put some lines there, and Jenna managed to engage a man from the coffin club to put the lines up for her. Now what was his name again? Jenna tried to remember but conceded it would come to her at another time. Probably a most inconvenient time.

With the washing hung Jenna made her way to the inside and wrote a list of the few things she needed. Some fruit, milk, coffee, dinner, meat for tomorrow night, salad greens, eggs, and with her list complete she headed into town to the supermarket.

The supermarket was not busy so Jenna got around without interruption, and found herself heading to the local roast hut for her dinner. Roast hut dinners were not only filling they we economical. Jenna bought the small one and there was never any left over so there was no waste. Weekly roasts no longer happened as they had when she and Adam were raising their children. Sunday was the Roast meal night when they would all be together. That thought Jenna as she took her plate down from the cupboard before plating her roast meal was decades ago and another lifetime it seemed to her now, but then when she was with her family the traditional roast meal night had emerged with each of her three children.

Having enjoyed her dinner and her first day home with her washing not only done, but also hanging on the line, Jenna made her way to her bed thinking not for the first time, why do we cling on to traditions when they are just something that we have made? And why do people make such a thing of them? They are a comfort she conceded although she couldn't validate how they were as she descended quickly into sleep.

The alarm woke her on time at nine o'clock and Jenna got up showered, dressed and made her way to the kitchen to organise some breakfast, and her first cup of tea for the day.

Sitting at her table some time later have eaten her breakfast and still drinking her tea she looked at the view which was calming. The grass was lush and green. There was barely no wind. The sky was blue. A true April day with a slight chill in the air. Mental note to self put your cardigan on before walking over to Anne's, and before Jenna knew it, it was indeed time to leave for Anne's.

The walk to Anne's was pleasant and Jenna was pleased she had decided to wear her cardigan. Anne opened the door to her and threw her arms around her saying "I have missed you."

Jenna was quite surprised by this overt demonstration of affection which was quite uncharacteristic of Anne. Jenna smiled saying "I've missed you too. It's funny isn't it even when you are busy and in new surroundings your mind travels to the places and people you have left at home?"

"Yes. I know what you mean. When I was on the cruise at Christmas especially at meal times when I could choose whatever I wanted, and it was there all laid out in front of me, I would think often of what would I be cooking at home, and Louisa who was used to cruising would get quite cross with me and say you can come back for more later if you want. You know giving me the hurry up. Then there was the menu at night at the end of a busy day of relaxation, walking, reading and whatever else, to have to go over a menu and make choices."

"I'll bet that was very tough on you Anne. Very tough indeed."

"Different not tough." Anne said.

"Do you think you will go on a cruise again?" Jenna asked Anne.

"I would love to. Would you consider joining me Jenna?"

"A Cruise. Well I have never seen myself going on a Cruise, but then I never saw myself going on a plane either so perhaps that is something to think about."

"Now tell me. How are the children? And more to the point how are the expectant mothers?" Anne asked and with those two questions posed the answers took way longer than Jenna had imagined and before they knew it their morning was coming to an end.

Jenna had asked what had happened in the township while she was away, and was told not a lot, although there had been a spate of arsons in close succession. Anne gave Jenna her mail and they agreed to catch up again later in the week when Jenna had caught up on herself.

"Jet lag I suspect" Jenna said as she began to feel quite tired, "time for a Nana nap."

"You know Jenna when I look at you I never see you as old enough to be a Nana even with your hair greying."

"My hair Anne has been greying from my early twenties I have chosen not to colour it anymore that's all. I will phone you in a couple of days. Thank you for collecting the mail and flyers and checking on my place. My indoor plants have never looked so vibrant. Oh and just before I go, I picked you up a little something. Yes here it is." Jenna said handing the jewellery box to Anne which Anne opened immediately, a large smile followed, "Oh Jenna it is quite lovely." She said looking at the mother of pearl necklace as Jenna made her way through the opened door and down the driveway towards her home, so she would be in good time for the phone call she was expecting from Jean.

"Hello Jenna." Jean said brightly, "I was just wondering how you are placed early June?"

"I am placed quite firmly at home at this stage I believe Jean." Jenna answered with a giggle.

"I was wondering if I could come for a break." Jean asked.

"Absolutely. Is everything all right Jean?"

"Yes mostly. I just have these days when the walls seem to come crashing in on me. They don't happen all the time you understand. It's just..."

"I do understand. It is grief Jean and grief I'm afraid is a process." Jenna told her with an understanding tone. "Do you want me to come down and get you?"

"Oh no. No. Cyril and Joy have a silver wedding to attend in Hamilton, then they are going up to the Bay of Islands for a few days. They have offered to drop me off on their way and pick me up again if that is all right with you."

"A bit like lost and found then?" Jenna asked, to which they both laughed, and continued chatting until Jean finally got around to giving Jenna the dates. "Now if anything changes don't feel you are locked into this Jenna just phone me and let me know. I won't take offense. You will be down again or I can make my way up on another occasion." Jean said just prior to ending the call.

Jenna made her way to her diary and trusted calendar hanging on her kitchen wall and wrote the dates in. June she thought and we are nearly through April already.

"It will be nice to have some company for a few days won't it?" she asked the hat walking passed on the way to her office with her diary in hand.

No sooner had Jenna put the diary down on top of her desk than she heard a knock at the front door. Making her way back along the hallway to the door she looked through the small window and saw a Police car on her driveway.

Opening the door she said "Constable Fraser how may I be of assistance?"

"Mrs Mitchell we are advising people to be vigilant. Now I know you are back off the road, but if you see or hear anything or anyone please let us know. We have had a spate of arsons around the town over the last few months and we are asking people to make sure the petrol, diesel any flammables they have are locked away. Here is my card." He said handing the card to Jenna and he promptly returned to his vehicle started it and drove down the driveway.

No sooner had Jenna got back inside than the phone rang "Hello Jenna.

I have just had the police here." Anne said.

"Me too."

"They are visiting everyone along this stretch of road. Do you think we are in danger?" Anne asked sounding quite frightened.

"No but how about I come along and we check your place together?"

"Oh thank you Jenna." She said and Jenna got her keys, locked up and made her way to Anne's. As they were checking the property including the shrubbery they came across two well placed petrol cans, that Anne said "These are not ours. I mean mine. Do you think we should phone the police?"

"Yes I do and we will leave them exactly where they are."

Anne went inside and phoned the number she had been given and within an extremely short time Constable Fraser appeared.

"So you are sure they are not yours?"

"Quite sure." Anne said.

"Your husband wouldn't have put them there?"

"Late husband" Anne informed him, "and why would he put them there? He had a double garage with shelves and designated areas for all manner of things. Our petrol can is where it should be and we only ever had the one." Anne said.

"Right. Well I will take them with me then. May get some prints off them." He said trying to pick them up. "Did you know they are full?" He asked.

"No I did not." Anne said, "Jenna said we shouldn't touch them."

"Mrs Brown do you have somewhere you can stay for a night or two? I don't mean to frighten you."

"But whoever put them there is intending to come back at some point and get them." Anne said.

"Anne can stay with me." Jenna said. "Anne get a few things together and we will lock up and walk back to my place together."

Constable Fraser took the two petrol cans he had put into large bags to his car and continued on his way.

CHAPTER TWO

Jenna was going through her day like any other, and was on track with her list of jobs in town completed, when she returned home to a blinking phone indicating someone had phoned her in her absence and had left her a message. Thinking it was probably her friend Jean who was normally was due to phone later on that day, Jenna carried on unloading her car, and putting things away. Jean knows Tuesday is bill, and groceries day she thought while she put the jug on, and continued putting the last of the groceries away, the receipts in her filing cabinet in her office, and then got changed into her house clothes ready to do some weeding in the garden later that afternoon.

Jenna had her cup of tea and was about to head out to begin the weeding when she remembered the phone message waiting for her attention. Lifting the handset and listening to the message Jenna began to feel quite sick in the stomach so much so that she physically swayed, and then found herself grabbing hold of the kitchen bench top to steady herself.

Firstly the call was not from Jean as Jenna had expected, and secondly the news left on the answer machine was not anywhere on Jenna's horizon. It was the phone call that in one instant changed the present forever, the future to one of uncertainty and anxiousness for Jenna, and revived a parallel past, which was now once again colliding with Jenna's present, and for quite some time Jenna stood frozen to the spot not knowing what to do.

When she finally managed to collect herself she listened to the message again, wrote down the number, then promptly phoned her lawyer Mr. Benton.

It was five o'clock and Mr. Benton known for his punctuality normally would be leaving his office now, but fortunately for Jenna he answered the phone and when she began to tell him about the message he said kindly "Give me the phone number Jenna and I will phone him for you and see what I can arrange. A meeting with him perhaps where we both attend?"

"Oh thank you. Yes." Jenna responded feeling a sense of gratitude overwhelming her.

"Now you get on with the rest of your day and don't dwell I will be in touch." And with that Mr. Benton was gone and Jenna felt a peace beginning to descend upon her. No matter what happens now she thought, I am not having to deal with it alone. With a sense of purpose Jenna went to the gardening shed to get her gardening tools and she set about weeding with some vigour.

Once the gardening was finished Jenna put her tools and gloves away in the garden shed, went to the back door, removed her shoes and placed them on the shelf in the porch, before entering the laundry, washing her hands and continuing on to the kitchen, passing the Hat and saying "poached eggs on toast for dinner. Something light will be quite adequate don't you think?" Knowing the silent confirmation from the Hat would justify her decision.

Putting on the radio while she prepared her dinner their song 'Of All the Girls I've Loved Before' sung by Julio Iglesias began playing. The irony, the timing, the absurdity of it, "You absolute rotter Adam Mitchell. Liar. Cheat. Coward." She heard herself saying with such vehemence she literally had to catch her breath, followed by the thought, so much for the forgiveness process being successful, and then she promptly burst into tears, and sobbed without constraint of any kind for what seemed to her to be quite some time, until there seemed to be no tears left.

Surprisingly Jenna slept soundly through the night and was wakened by the ringing of the telephone. "Good morning Jenna," Mr. Benton said "I have made an appointment for one o'clock today I will be in Cambridge on another matter and was wondering if you could meet me there?"

"Yes. Yes of course."

"Very good. The lawyer is Craig Somers and his address is," Mr. Benton was saying while Jenna was furiously trying to find the paper and pen she normally had on her bedside table.

"Thank you." She said as she got herself out of bed and hung the phone up. Seeing the paper and pen on the floor she picked them up and noted down the address. Looking over at her clock she saw she had slept through to ten o'clock. Some people might have said that maybe the release of three years of being civil and not upsetting others by the way of many tears was good for the soul, but Jenna was not thinking about any of that, she was on her way to shower and dress and make her meeting at eleven o'clock with the coffin group. She was in regular attendance there now and enjoyed the group. She and Pamela were helping a family getting a coffin ready for a much loved grand-dad who had been given only weeks to live. The group was very good like that. All hands rallied for those who needed help and support and assistance just as they had with Roy Hazlett's coffin. Jean had found solace in that. The grandchildren were arriving today to put their artwork on the coffin for their grand-dad.

Jenna arrived just a few minutes before time and found some of the grandchildren milling around in the car park.

"Hello. I believe we are here to do some art for your grand-dad." They nodded looking quite anxious, that will be me at one o'clock Jenna thought but said "No need to be anxious follow me. Oh good here is Pam. Pam runs the show. Pam the grandchildren." Jenna said by way of introduction "Hello." said Pam. "We were expecting a few more of you?" she asked.

"There has been a glitch. I am Sean, this is Pru, Emily, and Bud." He said pointing to each one. "We have the designs the others want and some of their memorabilia. That's the word isn't it?"

"Why can't you say items like a normal person?" Bud said.

"Good. Well as I said I am Pam, this is Jenna, and there are a couple of men here John and Paul, who have put your grand-dads coffin together, and done the base painting ready for you to do your bits so we are all here to help. Jenna and I will show you the material you can choose for the lining."

"Like in the Bible. John and Paul." Emily said

"Well I don't know if they would see it quite like that" Pam said with a smile "But yes there certainly is a John and Paul in the bible and they helped people too."

In no time at all the small group had put themselves into two groups of two. Pru and Bud concentrated on the lining and the memorabilia and how to arrange that while Sean had begun drawing the designs on the coffin and Emily was concentrating on the design of the family tree on the inside of the coffin lid where they were to paste some of the memorabilia. In no time at all Jenna found herself having to bid her farewell to make her appointment in the next town.

Fortunately there was minimal traffic and Jenna was praying for a park near to the lawyers' office once she had located the office of course, and found a free parking area literally around the corner.

Taking a deep breath she stepped out of her car, locked it and made her way to the office where Mr. Benton was waiting also.

"How are you Jenna?"

"I am very angry Mr. Benton which I can see surprises you, but it also surprises me, when really we should not be surprised by my reaction at all. One is still allowed to react to events isn't one? Or has that right gone now as well?" Jenna asked him.

Mr. Benton having known Jenna a very long time and having worked with her on many things was quite saddened by the defensive tone Jenna was using, coupled with her body language which he found quite concerning, "perhaps we should step out for a moment. Mr. Somers is running a little late." Mr. Benton said leading the way. Once outside he said "I have to say, this Jenna Mitchell is a new one to me."

"Me too." Jenna replied. "I thought I had handled all the Adam stuff. There was the house sale, purchase, lack of money, them being taken care of, life insurance policies of which only one was paid out to me and I knew there were two. You did your best but that is out there somewhere. You don't buy two then only find one now do you? and you said to let it go, Adam probably didn't get around to buying it. As we couldn't find the policy number or any other information I did just that rolled over like a well-trained dog and let it go. Just like I got married. Had children. Allowed the Boarder the work mate of Adam's into our home. Just do it Jenna and Jenna did it, and all the while Adam was out doing his own thing, and now here again I am being told something and expected to do it. Well I am not going to." Jenna said with such determination that it was Mr. Benton who the one was taking the deep breath.

"Let us see how much information Mr. Somers has shall we. I know what he has been directed to do, but that doesn't mean."

"And there are the children. Selfish man. It isn't their fault." Jenna said feeling overwhelmed by a sudden sense of compassion.

"Let's go in now shall we. I will be with you Jenna. We are in this together." Mr. Benton said kindly.

"Really? You know we have worked through a lot of things together over the years but in reality I am the one who has had to live with the consequences of them on a daily basis while you, as you should get on with your life and help your other clients as a part of your life so we are not really in this together. You are here today and we will have to work through this obviously, you will send the bill for your time and services and then you will get on with your life and leave me to make the best of mine." Jenna said with a finality that jolted them both. They both knew it was true. They both knew there was a rocky time ahead. They both knew there would be tension and heartache and many people affected, but what Jenna didn't know right in this very moment was that there would be revelations, and change, closure and new beginnings affecting the lives of the people she loved.

"Mr. Somers can see you now." The Receptionist said. "Second door on the left." And with that Jenna walked towards an unknown future.

Mr. Somers was very young. That is what struck Jenna in the first instance in fact he looked barely out of university. "Craig Somers" he said "You must be Mr. Benton and you are obviously Mrs Mitchell. Take a seat."

"To where?" asked Jenna receiving a very disapproving look from Mr. Benton who found no humour in her questions at all.

"Yes it is one of those things isn't it. What we are meaning doesn't quite line up with what is said. Much like have a seat. Who wants to have extra seats? Now to matters at hand. Primarily the children Joshua Duane Mitchell eight years of age, and Emma Claire Mitchell seven years of age.

"Yes regarding the children. You left a message that Jenna is to pick them up from the school or a friend's home?"

"Yes they are with the Anderson's. Suzanne and Rod Anderson and their two children Rachael who is seven and in the same class as Emma, and Jeremy who is nine. As I said on the phone the funeral is tomorrow at three o'clock and as Guardian you need to make arrangements with the Anderson's to pick the children up and rehouse them.

"Yes well that's the thing. Jenna had no idea she was their Guardian."

"Well that's not true. Let me see. Yes here it is in the file. November twenty second last year Julia expressly said that

Jenna Mitchell was the children's Guardian, gave me your details and assured me you had agreed to it."

"Yes that is all well and good Mr. Somers but Jenna knew nothing about it. That is my point. That is why I am here."

"Yes but you see Jenna Mitchell is named. The Anderson's were named. Julia Mitchell had everything organised."

"Julia is not a Mitchell." Jenna said. "Why on earth would Julia name me as Guardian? It makes no sense."

"As their grandmother it makes perfect sense."

"I am not their grandmother." Jenna said getting visibly upset. "How long have you been out of law school? Don't they teach you to check your facts?"

"If I may. Jenna perhaps you could go and have a coffee at the cafe over the road and take a few moments while Mr. Somers and I talk?" Mr. Benton said "By your leave Jenna." He added with an assertiveness Jenna had never heard before. Completely flabbergasted by what had been revealed she said "I thought I had left all this sorry mess behind. By your leave indeed. I have no intention of leaving. Now let's get on shall we. Why don't we start with who I am? I am the widow of the late Adam Mitchell to whom I was married. Julia was his mistress. They were never married. They had two children together of which I knew nothing. Not of the affair, the children, nothing until they turned up at Adam's funeral and." Jenna was interrupted by Mr. Somers.

"Mrs. Mitchell I think a coffee would be a very good idea. This brings up a number of legal matters that may need to be raised and discussed with Mr. Benton. If you could come back in let's say twenty minutes? Half an hour? I would be most grateful." Mr. Somers said who was visibly shaken.

Looking at Mr. Somers and Mr. Benton Jenna knew that there had been a shift, a dynamic change to the events at hand," Very well. I can see this changes things for you Mr. Somers. I trust you will both be able to bring me up to speed on my return?"

"I can't promise you that Jenna but I think we will have a better platform to work from." Mr. Benton said.

Jenna left the two legal minds to work out whatever it was they needed to, and went to find the cafe. Once there she ordered a Toasted Sandwich from the menu board and an Iced Chocolate, two things she hadn't had tasted or consumed in years.

Sitting watching people getting on with their daily business Jenna was struck with the fragility and uncertainty of life and the way it plays out. Like a pebble on a pond the ripples move the water out and about. For the observer it is restful to watch, for the water it is a major disruption to its current state. How apt Jenna thought and was interrupted by the arrival of her Iced Chocolate. "Your Sandwich isn't far away," the waitress informed her. "Thank you." Jenna said and picking up the parfait spoon to stir the Iced Chocolate.

The half hour passed very quickly and Jenna soon found herself back in the presence of Mr. Somers and Mr. Benton who both looked in need of something much stronger than the Iced Chocolate and Toasted Sandwich Jenna had just consumed.

CHAPTER THREE

Jenna had not been the only one surprised and shocked by what Mr. Benton had found out. Julia had been living as Mrs. Mitchell for the entire time she had been having the affair with Adam. Julia had presented the life insurance policy Adam had told Jenna about as Mrs. J Mitchell having contacted the Insurance Company claiming a mistake in the name had occurred. Changing Jenna to Julia and other relevant details. There was however the issue of the children who would now be put into the care of the State if no suitable solution was found.

Mr. Somers had contacted the Anderson family and they were happy to have the children while matters were being addressed. They could stay with the Anderson's for up to six weeks as they were to be holidaying together in the term break, which had been arranged the previous year.

Mr. Benton agreed the status quo would be more beneficial for the children. Mr. Benton and Jenna went to see the children. They did know Jenna. They had met a few times before.

Jenna attended the funeral with them and the Anderson's who were lovely and very understanding of the situation. They too had been told Jenna was the children's grandmother.

While they were walking back to their cars Jenna said to Mr. Benton "I think Julia was a piece of work." To which Mr. Benton replied "Well we will get to the bottom of it. They are lovely children it is such a shame."

"Yes it is. It is not their fault is it? None of it?"

"It wasn't your fault either Jenna." Mr Benton said giving her hand a squeeze.

Later that evening Jenna was talking to David about the situation who was initially shocked, then surprised at Jenna's apparent lack of concern for the children. "They are blood mum. They can't go into care."

"They are not my blood." Jenna said. "You know David as a parent you support, love, pick up the pieces of your children's lives where needed. These are not my children."

"Adam was your husband."

"Adam was a cheat and a liar who lived a double life. That life had nothing to do with me and that includes their children." Jenna said followed by, "I am ending this call. If you can't see that I have no responsibility here."

"All I see are our brother and sister in need."

"Fine you have them then." Jenna said and pushed the red button which concluded the call.

David who was in their office in his home in Australia, had been joined by his wife Deanna during the call, and was angry with his mother, looking to Deanna for support he was shocked when she said, "I don't know who you think you are speaking to your mother like that, or why you expect your mother to fix everything? Choices were made without her input. I think she is being very reasonable. Your siblings, no half siblings are your blood not hers, and your father is responsible for that not her. I think you need to contact your full siblings and see what they have to say. This is not for your mother to resolve David. Then you need to call your mother back and apologise." Deanna said leaving the room.

David sat stunned. He was stunned on multiple fronts he realised. Front one was he did expect his mother to step up and take the children and fix it. Front two was Deanna had not only taken his mother's side but told him off and demanded he apologise to his mother. Front three he had no idea what to say to his siblings and hoped that his mother had already spoken to them. Front four how would they manage two more children into their own growing family with Deanna having a baby and their two teenage children already.

David called his sister Karla who also lived in Australia. "I have put you on speaker phone Bryce is here with me."

"Karla have you been speaking with Mum?" he asked.

"Not for a week or so. Is something up?"

"More than something." David replied and told them what he knew. The next call was to Vincent and his wife Brittany in Canada who were just as shocked as Karla and Bryce had been, and it was only after David had ended the call with them that he realised he was in a state of shock himself, both by the news he had received, and he was also embarrassed when he realised that the rest of the family had all shared concern for their mum Jenna and how was she? How is she coping? What can we do to support her as well as sharing concern for the children? Karla was prepared to have the children, even though they were awaiting the arrival of their first born baby and Vincent said characteristically "Give us some time and I will get back to you." With Brittany adding "How much time do we have?" to which David had no idea, in fact David had to admit he had no ideas at all, and now felt he had completely failed on all fronts, or so it seemed to him in that moment.

With a sleepless night under his belt and a busy day underway at work he scheduled some time for the afternoon and phoned the family lawyer Mr. Benton. Having spoken with him he ascertained a time line, and some other facts, and early that evening he phoned Karla and Vincent back. As stressful as it was to relate to them the information he had been given regarding the children, the most challenging of all calls had yet to be made and where did he start. "How is mum today?" Vincent asked him. "I have no idea. We didn't." David started to say. "You expect mum to have them don't you?" Vincent said. "Really David. You know Mum used to say you were the settled one. You knew what you were going to do for a career, how many children you would have, who you would marry. She should have said you were the self-absorbed one." Brittany interrupted "David, Vincent and I are looking into some options can you email Mr. Benton's details through to us please."

"Of course." David said so cross with his brother he didn't bother to ask what the options were they were looking into, seeing Vincent as the same opinionated prat he had been growing up, always trying this and that, never sticking to anything. That was then of course. David had to concede that Vincent had certainly stuck with the Architectural stuff, and the love of his life as he described Brittany even though he had left a wake of beautiful women on his journey to finding her.

With his reminder beeping David resumed his work and decided to phone his mother when he got home from work which he did. He had no choice really, the moment he entered the house Deanna said "Have you decided what time you will phone your mother?" Which David had and rang her right there and then. The phone in New Zealand rang and rang, before finally going onto the answer phone "Hi this is Jenna leave me a message, have a great day and I will get back to you."

Sometime later Deanna appeared, "How did that go?"

"It didn't." David snapped at her.

"Would you like me to speak to her?"

"No Deanna. I would like her to pick up the phone." David said.

"Perhaps she is tied up with the funeral. She did say she would be there today didn't she?"

"Oh yes. I forgot about that, and with the time difference."

"David I think you had better take a moment and get yourself together. Dinner in ten minutes and we had better talk to our children about what has happened. They know Josh and Emma too."

"Yes of course. I. Well I have been a bit caught up. Do you know Vincent told me today that he and Karla thought of me as being self-absorbed?"

"Did they?" Deanna said as she returned to the kitchen to finish dishing up dinner.

After dinner David and Deanna told Richard and Stephanie about their niece and nephew Josh and Emma and how their mum had passed away.

"What will happen to them?" Richard asked.

"We don't know at this stage." David said.

"Could we have them?" Stephanie asked. "There wouldn't be such a big gap with the new baby coming then would there." She stated always the pragmatist

David thought, the deal with this now and just get on with the next thing, a trait her uncle Vincent exhibited often.

"We don't know what arrangements have been made as yet. There seems to be some gaps that need to be filled." Deanna said.

"But who will be with them at the funeral?"

"Your Nan is with them today."

"What about tomorrow and the days after that?" Stephanie asked beginning to have tears rolling down her cheeks.

"They are staying with friends of theirs. They are being looked after." David said finding himself getting emotional as well.

"It will work out then. Nan will find a way." Richard said.

"It is not for your Nan to find a way Richard. It is quite complicated." Deanna said trying to explain.

"Nan always does the right thing." Richard said which given the circumstances was a very naive thing to say and proved that although he was now eighteen he still had a lot of growing up to do , but then David had reacted the same way and he was Richard's father.

"I think we need to concentrate on the things we can do right now. I have a phone number if you would like to speak with Josh and Emma?" Deanna said.

"What would we say?" Richard asked.

"How's it hanging would hardly be appropriate now would it?" Stephanie said and proceeded to make the call. "Hello can I speak with Josh and or Emma please it is Stephanie their aunt." After a short break David heard Stephanie say "I have put you on speaker phone, Richard is here too. How are you both?" and with that the conversation between them flowed for a good fifteen minutes before Stephanie handed the phone to David "I believe Nana Jen was with you today? I'm sure that was a big help." And it occurred to Deanna that for all his drive and certainty in business matters, in his personal life David had cracks like everyone else, and like everyone else they enabled his uniqueness.

David waited a good hour before phoning his mother again and this time the call was answered. "Hello." Jenna said.

"Hello mum. Look about yesterday."

"After the gruelling day I've had, yesterday is but a distant memory. I am quite at a loss frankly. Those lovely children. Whatever her faults Julia has raised lovely children I will give her that. David I have to see Mr. Benton in the morning. I will contact you when I know more." She said and was gone.

Making her way to bed Jenna fell asleep almost as soon as her head hit the pillow, her last thoughts on the children Josh and Emma who clinging on to her, had buried their mother that very afternoon.

It was with lots of tears shed and frantic waving that she left them with the Anderson's who were also still coming to terms with the facts of the matter.

Mr. Benton was very conciliatory when they met. "Let me start Jenna by saying I am profoundly sorry about the Life Insurance matter. I was dismissive of you at the time and only made cursory enquiries which wasn't adequate, and will be reflected in my bill if that is any consolation. Now Mr. Somers I believe has been manipulated somewhat by Julia, but I also think he has acted in good faith. He believed you were their grandmother because Julia used the term Nana Jen which is what Josh and Emma call you, and he extended that to mean you were their grandmother and that led Julia it would seem to take actions to make that relationship with you a reality, and further validate her claim of being Mrs. J. Mitchell.”

"What did she die of?” Jenna asked.

"An aneurysm.”

"What else have you found out?” Jenna asked him.

"I have had confirmed what I have known for a long time. You have raised outstanding children Jenna Mitchell and you should be rightly proud of them. They have all phoned me, and I think we may have a workable solution which will take some time, but will be in place within the six week period for Emma and Josh. ”

"I see and that would be? The workable solution?” Jenna prompted Mr. Benton.

"Oh yes. Vincent and Brittany are arranging to have the children with them in Canada. What do you think about that?”

"I don’t quite know what to think.” Jenna replied.

"Now the insurance. We have made calls to the company and there is paperwork to be done of course because an error was made, but Mr. Somers and I will take care of that. In short you will be reimbursed the full amount. There is still a sizable chunk untouched of the Life Insurance Policy which will go to you directly and then there is the Life Insurance that has been paid out to the children that was taken out for them independently by Julia quite some time ago now, so they will be well cared for, and all we have to do is address the Guardian status which was not agreed to by you. There is a process for that. But I suggest we wait until we hear back from Vincent and Brittany so we can go to the authorities with a family member who is able to become a Guardian."

"At this point anything is better for those children than becoming wards of the state." Jenna said.

So Jenna was to receive more money. Most people would be happy about that, but even when Jenna knew there was an additional life insurance policy out there she should have had to pay off everything, which would have reduced the financial stress at the time, nothing compensated her for the emotional harm Adam had inflicted, and still it was touching her, affecting her. "Money is not the be all and end all people think." She said.

"No Jenna it is not, but I fear it is the passing of years that brings that home. The reality for you now is that the Life Insurance Policy was originally taken out for you in your name and the company has all that. They have their own process to sort out. You know there is something to be said for handwritten documentation. On this occasion it is proof positive. So even though you are comfortable in a financial sense you are about to become significantly more so. Enjoy it. You have the means to do a lot more visitation of your family and I am quite sure you will continue to do good things with your means. You do have a knack for it you know."

Jenna though surprised Vincent and Brittany were seriously looking into having the children with them in Canada was relieved, but also felt this was the right solution. She also had no doubt that due process would enable things to go smoothly, and if she could help in any way she knew she would, even though they hadn't asked her to as yet.

Jenna had agreed to visit Josh and Emma on the weekend and give the Anderson's some time out. Jenna had thought that staying with the children in their home would be a practical thing to do, all their toys were there and they needed time at home. Jenna had been and sorted out the fridge, emptied the rubbish and decided where she would sleep making up the spare bed in the guest room, best to leave Julia's room as it was she had thought.

"Jenna?"

"Yes sorry I was miles away. I am looking after the children this weekend to give the Anderson's some family time." She said and explained to Mr. Benton what she had decided to do and why, and he just smiled.

CHAPTER FOUR

Jenna found her week days busy, and her weekend days even busier for quite some time. There were delays with the due process of both countries, and not surprisingly this led to Jenna being with the children more than she had envisaged. Once the six weeks were up Jenna moved into their family home to keep them near friends and attend the school holiday programme they had been enrolled in. Then there were the friends who were popping in and out, and the odd appointment that had been made late in the day, 'having to remember where to be, at what time, all that stuff, that I had let go of years ago" she told Jean in one of their afternoon calls "and do you know I had quite forgotten how much young children can eat and how often."

"I hope you are pacing yourself Jenna. You were looking tired when I came up and stayed with you and you were just doing the weekends then." Jean had said.

"They go to bed and I go to bed shortly after them. That seems to do the trick Jean."

"Dare I ask how the book is coming?"

"The book. Yes I have started the book but I am having some trouble with developing a flow just now. Brittaney will be over soon, and Vincent will be here two weeks after her, so I am hoping after that, I will get back to normal whatever that looks like now, and they will do whatever they need to I guess. You know Jean the great thing with technology is they have been able to Skype Vincent and Brittany a lot so they have been getting to know them better, and have seen where they will be living, and they are adapting to everything quite well. We do have the odd day where tears flow, but that is to be expected. I have got them grief counselling and that seems to be helping them. Once everything is settled I will come down for a visit and a break. I know we were aiming for October but who knows, the time frame may have to be kept open?"

"You know Jenna I've been thinking if Vincent and Brittany are here you could come in August. Yes it's winter and wet, but we could find things to do I am sure."

"Thank you Jean but I do have to get my place sorted. I am not saying no. I will think on it. Bye for now." Jenna said ending the call and getting afternoon tea ready for the two hungry children due in the door at any moment.

Jenna was reading the local paper while the children were getting ready to be picked for a friendly soccer match, when she came upon the crime section 'local man Peter Gillespie appeared in court today on eight counts of arson, four counts of theft of petrol, petrol cans, unlawful entry of property in two townships,' reading on she discovered he was to be held on remand with a court date of the fourth of August. So finally Jenna thought they have apprehended the arsonist who had been busy. No wonder there were gaps in between fires if two places were involved. The people of Cambridge and Te Awamutu could once again sleep easy.

Tania phoned later that evening "Jenna I am not putting you under any pressure, this is just a check to see how you are call."

"Do you know you are getting more like Judy every time I speak to you? The by any and all means to keep writers on track philosophy is rubbing off on you Tania. Just so you know I am up to chapter four and will email those chapters through to you for your editor. Who is?"

"Oh yes I meant to tell you, his name is Wade Morrison. He is in his forties and has been working abroad for some years. He is very efficient." Tania said.

"Efficient? Should I be scared? Is he one of those editors who is so efficient you have very little manuscript left?"

"I hope not. Well that has not been my experience to date. Now Jenna how are you really?"

"Tired and making the best of what can only be described as a cruel set of circumstances for all concerned."

"Honest as always. Baz and I are thinking of you and on that note Baz has asked if you and the kids would like to come for dinner Sunday night."

"Thank you Tania. Yes we would."

"Great dinner at six and we will get a DVD for the kids to watch. Ours will be in bed by seven and your two will be entertained while we catch up. I have missed you." Tania said and Jenna realised that she had missed Tania. Their relationship was more than just editor, slash publisher, slash colleague, slash friend, it was indescribable really, and if anyone had been asked to predict they would get along in their earlier days no one would have picked it, but they worked well together and understood each other well, and in spite of the professional distinctions and age difference, were good friends.

Bang went the back door, plop went the bags and two faces appeared in the kitchen with their eyes firmly fixed on the bench where their afternoon tea was ready.

"How was the programme today?" Jenna ventured.

"Do you think school and holiday programmes in Canada will be the same as here?" Joshua asked.

"School is school everywhere." Emma stated sounding much older than her seven years.

The afternoon proceeded with the children going to their soccer games, some television, showers, dinner, reading time and then bed. Even in the holidays there was not one night of the week where the children were not rushing off to something Jenna thought. Roll on Sunday what a blessing Jenna thought and found herself in bed by eight o'clock and fast asleep by eight thirty.

The following week with the school holidays now ended, Jenna walked with the children to school as she had a meeting with the Principal Mr. Simpson. Jenna was waiting outside his office when the school bell went off indicating the school day had officially started. Sitting and reflecting on a time which was long ago now but felt like yesterday, Jenna remembered being called by the Principal for a meeting about an incident Vincent had been involved in. Fearing Vincent had caused the incident and was yet again being disciplined Jenna having phoned Adam and being advised he couldn't go with her, Jenna arrived at the school feeling she was prepared for the ultimatum when the Principal came through the door with a very battered Vincent in tow and a very apologetic Principal at his side "As you can see he is a bit battered and bruised I'm afraid, our School Nurse has given him the once over but I think it best if you get your Doctor to have a look as well."

"What happened?" Jenna asked.

"A few boys set upon him it turns out that Vincent here has been the victim and not the bully at all. Fortunately the History teacher happened along at just the right time to see what happening from the beginning, but couldn't get to Vincent quickly enough before some damage was done. The boys involved have been sent home and meetings with their parents will be arranged. I am really very sorry about this Mrs. Mitchell. Vincent." The Principal said as she showed them through the outer door. Jenna and Vincent made their way to the car and

Vincent got into the front passenger seat while Jenna made her way around to the driver's door and once inside the car Vincent said "I told you and dad I wasn't the one causing trouble, and you chose to believe everybody else and now look at me" then promptly burst into tears.

Jenna went straight to the Doctor's room where Vincent was seen very quickly and sent to the hospital for X-Rays two broken ribs and a fractured wrist were revealed and Vincent spent several weeks doing school work at home. When he did return to school he returned to a situation where he ignored the bullies and kept himself in areas where there were lots of students. He retreated to the Library and although Vincent had never been a reader as such, he did discover books with pictures and diagrams and he began smiling again and the occasional laugh was heard from time to time as well. What was that Principals name? Jenna asked herself.

"Mrs. Mitchell. Mr. Simpson will see you now."

"Good morning Mrs. Mitchell. Please have a seat." Jenna nodded and smiled don't go there she thought.

"I take it you are wanting an update Mr. Simpson, and as I explained to you over the phone as soon as I know more I will tell you."

"That is why I have asked you to come in. I have finalized the paperwork with the authorities now and I would imagine that by the end of the month which is just three weeks away now all will be settled. I understand the carers soon to be new parents will be here by then."

"Yes. Brittany my daughter in law is due in two weeks and Vincent her husband, my son, will follow a week or so later." Jenna informed him.

"Well as I said our part is done. You know sometimes the wheels grind very slowly, sometimes they turn at an average speed, and there have been instances, not many I admit, but instances none the less where they have bolted to the finish line."

"What are you trying to tell me?" Jenna asked.

"The paperwork at this end is usually approved six weeks after submission. I submitted the paperwork last Thursday and I got confirmation it had been signed off today. So that part has taken a week."

"Yes I see. Thank you Mr. Simpson for letting me know."

"Mrs. Mitchell I don't have all the facts but if I could just say what a great job you have done with Joshua and Emma. I can't think of many people who would put their discomfort to one side as you have."

"So you know something of the situation then. Discomfort Mr. Simpson is not a word I would use for the situation, but if that is how you see it. Anyway the reality is Joshua and Emma are the tangible, living results, not the cause and they deserve to have the very best. It is Vincent and Brittany who should be given the credit they have literally turned their world upside down to accommodate the needs of Vincent's half brother and sister. I will phone them when I get home and leave them a message. Thank you again Mr. Simpson."

"Just before you go I thought I would let you know that Mrs. Murray and Miss Talbot will have an outline of where they are scholastically, and there will be contact details of course for the new teachers if they need any additional information. New country different schooling system, but the basics should be the same. Any questions you or your family have please don't hesitate to contact me." Mr. Simpson said with a kindly smile, and with that Jenna felt she had been dismissed.

Leaving the school grounds felt like coming to the end of a book. You know the end is just a page or two away but the conclusion isn't revealed yet and as Jenna walked along the footpath admiring the gardens, and making a mental note of the lawns that needed to be mowed and the weeding that could be done Jenna realised that the end was nearer than she had thought. She could feel it and she wasn't sure how she was feeling about it. She had gone from the I can't wait for this to be over, to the it will be over soon, to suddenly finding herself on the precipice and feeling quite apprehensive and sad, and just like that, spontaneously a tear rolled down her cheek. Surprising herself further Jenna heard these words "Pull yourself together Jenna Mitchell. It's your own fault. You knew that by looking after the children you would become attached." And with that admonishment she took a deep breath and continued her walk back to the house. On arrival at the house Jenna walked around to the back and unlocked the back door. She took her shoes off, and slipped her comfortable slippers on, closed the door locking the door behind her, before making her way through to the kitchen where she promptly filled the kettle and put it on. In no time at all the kettle was boiling. Even that would change Jenna mused. At her home she always put the jug on, but Josh and Emma had grown up with the kettle so the kettle it was here. The saying when in Rome Jenna thought had a very practical application here. With the water boiled and the coffee in the cup Jenna proceeded to make herself a very strong cup of coffee indeed before proceeding to the lounge where the laptop was set up for calling her children.

Making the call expecting to leave a video message Jenna was pleased and delighted to find that Brittany answered "Is everything all right?" she asked. "Oh yes" said Jenna "Very much so. I thought you would be in a state of deep sleep over there. Are you all right?"

"Yes I just got up to pee. Sorry use the toilet and I was thinking about you actually when I heard the call come in which is unusual because Vincent turns the computer off before retiring for the night. Any way what's up? You may as well tell me in person I am wide awake now."

"I have just got back from seeing the Principal he told me all his paperwork is complete which he says means the children will be able to come to you very soon indeed, and the time frame he mentioned was around three weeks.   End of the month. Do you need to write this down Brittany?"

"No I am so excited. I have all the instructions here. We will be getting dates in the next day or so I imagine. That is what we were told anyway. That once the school information was passed on we would be given dates. Oh thank you so much for letting me know. If I haven't heard anything in two days I will be making a phone call myself. You will be hearing from us soon. Love you." She said and then was gone. The smile not just on her lips but in her eyes, and across her whole face, confirmed the importance and the relevance of the last few weeks that meant more than just Josh and

Emma were being given a new start. Jenna felt a sense of absolute peace descend upon her and knew that before the end of the holidays she would once again be living in her own home with her hat and other treasures.

As she was about to Skype David to update him, she remembered "Mrs. Penbroke. That was the name of the Principal."

CHAPTER FIVE

Jenna found herself in a whirlwind of activity with Brittany's arrival, and children choosing what they would give to their friends when they left New Zealand. Jenna thought how very mature these two youngsters were and conceded not for the first time that their mother had given them life skills at a very young age. Skills at the time she was sure would not have been put to use so soon.

Not long after Brittany arrived over an evening meal Josh and Emma brought up the subject of what they would be taking with them and to Brittany's and Jenna's surprise when Emma announced "We have been talking it through for some time now and we think we should take just one or two special things and a few clothes, but choose some new things in Canada for our new home with you and Vincent."

Josh followed this with "If you have things for us already that's fine too, but if you haven't it doesn't have to be new stuff. So long as it is ours that will be fine as well."

"How old are you two again?" Brittany asked.

"Older than we were before Mum died." Emma said which summed the situation up for them completely.

"Shall we discuss this with Vincent then?" Brittany asked and the following morning the four of them discussed options and settled on some new, some existing and maybe some up-cycling for more permanent items.

Being their last week of school in New Zealand, and with their tickets booked for the following week to Canada, Brittany and Vincent had decided to save on Vincent's airfare, and put that money towards a family holiday when the next school holiday fell in Canada, and with shipping costs not needed that money would be put into the holiday fund as well. Josh and Emma thought this was a great idea and were very excited with the prospect of a family holiday, something that would be a new experience for them.

Once the children had left for school Brittany called Vincent back. "You don't think we are making a mistake by not having their furniture sent over?"

"No I think not listening to them would be the mistake. Look it's not just about the money. It will take weeks for their stuff to get here and having spoken with them they want a new start here. It is their way of coping Brit. It is something they have some control over."

"I don't know."

"Brit they will find things here that will make them comfortable and we will help them shift those things into their new life here with us. The up-cycling for drawers is a good idea. What are their drawers like there?" Vincent asked.

"Wooden. Older. Repainted and decorated."

"Exactly. What they have here will be what they are used to until they are ready to be a little more adventurous or their tastes change. Solid wood is a great idea. The redecorating can change as they grow but the drawers can remain." Vincent said in a mock authoritarian way which brought a smile to Brittany's lips. "How's mum coping?"

"She looks to be coping very well, although I don't really know to be honest, with the dates coming forward, and so much to do we are both busy. She was going to return to her home so I could spend time with the kids on my own before we left but Josh and Emma didn't want that, and with one thing and another it is better that she is still here. There is the business with the house of course and we need to decide whether to rent it out or sell it. The kids thought we could rent it furnished but"

"Mum. Vincent wants to know what you think about the house." Brittany said as she put the phone on speaker.

"I think you could rent it for six months to a year and then decide what's best. Don't you think you have quite enough on your plate right now?" Jenna asked.

"As always the voice of reason and logic. One step at a time. Oh my childhood lectures are coming back to haunt me." Vincent said. "You know Brit right now all I want is to meet you all at the airport, kiss you and scoop them up anything after that in this moment of time can just take care of itself."

"Impatient as ever I see. Perhaps I should have spent more time lecturing you." Jenna said winking at Brittany, then leaving the room for them to continue their conversation.

Over lunch Brittany asked Jenna "How are you Mum? I mean really. Even my parents are concerned for you. What you have done for them, for us, is massive and you will be on your own again and"

"You know Brittaney I really have no idea how I am. I see you with them and they with you, and hear the joy in Vincent's voice and where many people would feel burdened you two are radiating happiness, and beyond that right now I am not thinking about. Let's just get through the next week and a bit shall we.

One thing I do know is you will be helping me clear out the kitchen before you go. I don't intend being here once you have all gone. I will be dropping you all off at the airport and going home. Perhaps we should go in and see one of the real estate agencies about listing the house for rental before the children get home from school?"

"Okay." Brittany said and then the phone rang.

"Hello it is Suzanne Anderson speaking." Suzanne said.

"Hello Sue" Jenna said.

"Oh Jenna I am so glad I have caught you. The dinner for this Saturday I'm afraid I am going to have to cancel it. My brother and his family are moving in here temporarily they are making their way home from South Africa. Things have gone pear shaped I believe. Rod has said they are to stay here until they can find a rental. I am at a loss really."

"Well I think we may have a solution for you all." Jenna said and explained there was a fully furnished house available if they needed one.

Brittany sat with a grin spreading across her face. "What are you grinning about?"

"You and real estate. You have a gift for being in the right place at the right time."

"Not every time. Adam always took care of that. Anyway here I am making decisions and promising things when those decisions are really yours to make now aren't they?"

"Yes they are but the Anderson family are in a time of need and it is only fitting that we can meet their need, after all they stepped in for us didn't they?" Brittany said.

"Yes they did." Jenna replied.

"Have you ever wondered what the big picture really is? I mean we seem to get a picture or a bit of a picture. Life is like a jig saw sort of. Bits here and there and then all of a sudden you see this wonderful picture unfolding."

"Vincent told Adam that he had found an extraordinary woman, who saw beauty and unity in everything where other people saw chaos and confusion." Jenna told Brittany.

"And what did Adam say?" Brittany asked.

"He has it bad. This may be the one." And they exchanged a knowing look.

"I think I will have another go at the garden." Brittany said rising to get the gardening gloves she had left on the sideboard the day before. After putting the gloves on Brittany brushed the dirt off the sideboard and left through the back door. Jenna was both amused and annoyed by this action as the dirt had settled on the cream rug. Jenna shrugged and rose to get the carpet sweeper. The kids will be home soon she thought as she put the carpet sweeper away, then made her way to the kitchen. Looking through the back door she could see Brittany had almost finished her section of weeding. Yes the garden was looking cared for Jenna thought. The children were well and truly cared for and Jenna? Yes Jenna you will have to take care of you very shortly. All this is about to come to a rather abrupt end. Jenna told herself silently. Soon it will be back to you and the Hat. Jenna had known this for some time of course but the inevitability of it was fast approaching, and Jenna didn't really have a plan in place for the transition. Well any reasonable person would ask how could she. Cleaning the house out and putting it on the market would have been part of that plan but that option for now was no longer relevant. What to do? A knock at the front door stopped any more time wasting on these thoughts.

Jenna made her way to the front door and opened the door to a smiling Sue Anderson "Well I wasn't expecting to see you today." Jenna said.

"Nor was I expecting to visit today Mrs. Mitchell but I have a proposition for you. How would you feel about selling the house to us? As is where is. Once the children have vacated."

"Sell. I thought you needed a short term rental option?"

"Yes but then Rod said why don't we just buy it and they can stay as long or short as they like and we will have an extra property, a place where family can stay when they visit or whatever we like really, and I said really? I mean I didn't see that coming at all, but it makes sense somehow. I don't know how exactly." Sue said as she was making her way through to the kitchen arriving at the same time as Brittany who had just come in from the garden with her gloves already removed

Jenna was pleased to see. "Did I hear you offer to buy the house?" Brittany asked.

"Yes." Sue said.

"Time for a cup of tea? Coffee?"

"Just water for me." Sue said and with that Jenna got a glass down from the cupboard.

The conversation flowed easily until two children arrived home and Sue made a quick exit realising her children would be bounding into her own front yard very soon.

Josh and Emma grabbed an apple each from the fruit bowl and headed to their rooms.

"Well." Brittany said from renting to a sale in less than four hours. Definitely meant to be."

"You will have to phone the lawyer. Mr. Somers."

"Yes I will do that right now and make an appointment for tomorrow. They have offered market rate plus 30% for the contents. What do you think?"

"I think so long as the money is looked after it could be a good move, but I also think you should." Jenna was saying when Brittany finished the sentence for her by saying, "Discuss this with Vincent.

Will SKYPE him right now. He should be
stirring anyway."

With Vincent agreeing to the sale
and the figure mentioned, Brittany made
the appointment with Mr. Somers who had
a spot the following morning at nine
o'clock.

After a good night's sleep and with
the children at school Brittany and Jenna
arrived on time to see Mr. Somers the
lawyer they had of course both seen on
previous occasions. Brittany outlined the
offer made by the Anderson's and he
informed them that their lawyer had been
in touch the previous afternoon. "I must
say they are quite intent on the purchase.
I have some paperwork for you to sign
Mrs. Mitchell." Mr Somers said.

"Shouldn't it be Brittany that
signs?"

"No. You were named as the
guardian and even though that has
changed, you were the person to oversee
all legal matters which is different again,
so it is you I am afraid. Now given our
previous encounter I have taken the
liberty of arranging for your Mr. Benton to
be involved." With that the phone rang on
cue "Yes she is here I will pass you over."

Mr. Somers said handing the phone to Jenna who after a brief exchange found herself signing on the dotted line with the money to go into a trust for Josh and Emma that Mr. Benton had set up and that was that.

Brittany thanked Mr. Somers for all he had done and as they were about to walk out Mr. Somers said "Mrs. Mitchell would you mind giving me a moment?" Jenna stopped and nodded her agreement. "Thank you. I just want to say that the Life Insurance matter is being resolved, and I want you to know that your Mr. Benton has been a great help with it. It will be resolved soon but he will be in touch with you about that."

"Thank you Mr. Somers." Jenna said and left to join Brittany by the car.

"I feel like a very large cup of Hot Chocolate." Jenna said.

"Hot Chocolate before ten o'clock in the morning are we celebrating or commiserating?" Brittany asked.

"I don't know about you but I am definitely walking to the cafe around the corner, and I think I will add a white chocolate and raspberry muffin to the tray."

"Goodness." Said Brittany knowing that Jenna normally had a savoury scone if she ordered a food item at all, and began walking with her. "Perhaps we could share the muffin?" Brittany asked as they entered the cafe.

"Only if you are prepared to share the caramel slice we both know you are going to buy." Jenna said as Brittany got a tray and put two plates on it.

While they waited for their drinks to arrive Jenna said "I am going to miss you Brittany."

"And the children of course." Brittany added. "I will miss spending time with you too." Brittany said.

"No you won't Brittany you literally will not have the time for that. We have just a few days left now and in a way I am glad the house has been sold. It means complete closure of a chapter that…" Jenna stopped talking to catch her breath, "Brittany when I was emptying some clothes in Julia's drawer I found Adam's great grandmother's brooch and a brooch from her grandmother. They are in this envelope with the children's name on them. I want you to keep them in a safe place for them. The card inside mentions they are to have them on their twenty first birthdays." Jenna said handing Brittany the envelope.

"I see, now I get why you need the Hot Chocolate you are starting the goodbye process."

"I need you to look after them Brittany. Put them in a safe or something when you get home. They are worth a lot of money. I have had them valued and have the certificate of valuation here to go with them."

"Not just trinkets then?"

"Oh no."

"Are you sure about this Jenna. I mean Julia's grandmother I can understand but Adam's?"

"You know Julia really believed she was Adam's wife and these are Adam's children. This is as it should be. They were the parents and they made this decision."

"They made other decisions too which were."

"Whatever feelings well up now Brittany, and I have to say being in the current situation they have been welling up far more than I would have liked, but with all that put to one side, I know I cannot change the past. I can move on with my future knowing I did a bit in a time of need and I have survived it. In fact there are bits I have enjoyed in spite of myself. Mr. Somers will have things in place that enable you and Vincent to have access to money the children will need while making sure the children are financially secure. We don't want you two worrying about money."

"We haven't discussed money that is something that always turns up when you need it, so neither of us have been worried about that." Brittany said and with a smile she added "Right on Cue here comes your Hot Chocolate." Once the drinks were on the table Brittany raised her latte and said "A toast to an amazing woman, we hope to have you come to us Christmas next year how does that sound?"

"That sounds like something to look forward to."

"I will tell Josh and Emma you are coming then." Brittany said.

CHAPTER SIX

With Josh, Emma and Brittany home in Canada with Vincent, and the children's possessions sorted out, Jenna had found herself once again at home with her trusted companion the Hat, and as much as Jenna enjoyed her own company she was feeling very unsettled which surprised her. Thoughts of relief is what she had expected to join her, but they seemed elusive, and life seemed quite flat.

The coffin club had new people attending now so Jenna didn't really know them at all. Jean had needed ankle surgery after she fell at her local supermarket so weekly phone calls had ceased for the interim, and with the gardens tidied Jenna was beginning to wonder what she was going to do. Jenna's pity party was interrupted by a knock on her front door and fortunately Anne her neighbour was there to deliver Jenna the solution "Jenna I am surprised you have not been over for coffee. I hope you are not avoiding me. I just thought this morning it is high time we two went to a movie and had dinner somewhere, so I have decided that whatever you were going to do today, you are cancelling it. Nothing planned? All the better. Now get changed we leave in thirty minutes. I will pick you up." Anne said and was gone as quickly as she had arrived.

Jenna was quite stunned by this. Anne had certainly become more open and pragmatic since the death of her husband, but this was absolutely outside the parameters Jenna was accustomed to where Anne was concerned. "I go away for a few months and the neighbour's become someone else it would seem." Jenna said passing by the Hat.

As it turned out the rest of day was lovely and Anne once she and Jenna were seated in the movie theatre apologised for her authoritarian approach. "What must Jenna have thought I said to myself as I unlocked my back door? Going over there demanding that she spend time with me. I must apologise I told myself and now I have. Really Jenna I don't know what came over me." Anne said. "I have missed you being there. I know it sounds silly but honestly."

"I have missed you too Anne and I am not going to accept your apology, because there is absolutely no need for one. I was remiss by not calling on you earlier. I have been meaning to, but the fact is I have been in a bit of a void."

"Well of course you have. You are grieving Jenna. You are still grieving the loss of your husband and the marriage you thought you had, and now the loss of the children you have been minding. I mean it is not as if they are along the road and you can pop in. And going back even further not as if you were a grandparent to them in the first place. I mean they aren't your grandchildren so it is no wonder having put all that to one side and coming back to your house and being on your own and alone again. I get it completely. It will take a bit of time for your world to return to its rightful axis." Anne said insightfully. And right on cue the screen came to life with advertisements, including the one reminding people to go to the candy bar for refreshment which always amused Jenna because people were well seated and comfortable by then and the movie was about to start so why would you? She thought and then saw two people leaving the theatre to do just that.

The movie and dinner were a triumphant success and they agreed to repeat the occasion the following week with Jenna choosing the movie. This wouldn't be difficult as they had both wanted to see another movie that was playing at the same time. Jenna smiled as she was dropped off and walked along to her bedroom passing the Hat she said, "Well that is one day of the week taken care of, can you do something about the other six please. No make that five even I deserve a day off."

Having changed into her nightgown Jenna made her way to the kitchen to fill the jug up for the following morning when she noticed the blinking light on her phone. Raising the handset from its cradle she listened to the message that had been left "Hi Jenna it's Tania. I need you to come into the office next Tuesday at ten o'clock. I know I said I would be in touch later and I am sorry about this but later seems to have arrived earlier than expected with an unexpected opportunity. Oh dear you are rubbing off. Call me when you get this would you?"

Jenna rang Tania immediately "Tania, Jenna here. What exactly were you trying to say in your message?"

"Yes it was a bit garbled. I was a bit scrambled. The thing of it is this. They want you to do book signings in Australia. Your last three books have gone viral over there."

"Australia. I have only just got home and I have an engagement next Thursday."

"Yes I will work around that. See you Tuesday then to finalise the details." Tania said as she hung up the phone. Jenna was quite shocked by this remembering conversations of a similar vein with her previous publisher Judy. Then the phone rang "I meant to ask how

you are? Sorry I'm a bit under the pump."
Tania said.

"I suggest you get Baz that lovely
husband of yours to take a course in
hydraulics, so he can help to alleviate that
problem, and get the pump off you. I
nearly called you Judy."

"Yes well on that. I can see why she
was so curt if that's the right word. At
times." Tania said.

"I am adjusting and not too well.
Today has been one of my better days I
have to say. I will see you Tuesday at ten
o'clock hopefully we will have time for a
proper catch-up then." Jenna said before
putting the handset back into the cradle.

Ready for bed Jenna found comfort
between her cotton sheets and laid her
head back on her goose down pillow her
last thoughts of the evening were "You
wanted to fill your days in. They will
become busy again by the sounds of it,"
and with that thought a deep slumber
overtook her. Jenna slept soundly and in
the morning she woke to the realisation
that she had received exactly what she
had told the Hat she wanted so having
showered and dressed she made her way
to the kitchen and as she passed the Hat

she said "I suppose I have you to thank for that."

Looking through her dining room window Jenna decided she would drive into town and take a leisurely stroll around the gardens and maybe sit on one of the memorial seats and just observe life unfolding in front of her eyes. There were always birds there making themselves busy ferreting for bugs to eat. Yes she thought I will definitely spend a relaxing time there, as she rose to seek out her comfortable walking shoes.

The air was damp and the day overcast but there were varying shades of green from the trees, and a multitude of colour moving in and around her. Gone were the days of people wearing brown or black in the colder months, and so too it seemed were the days of people staying indoors on overcast days. Jenna was watching the changing of the guard you could say. People seemed to arrive in shifts almost do their turn around the garden and then depart leaving space for others, who on this day were arriving all the time.

Jenna's eye was drawn to an older woman who had just sat down and a much younger man who was standing in front of her. The older woman looked familiar but Jenna couldn't put a name to her just at that moment, she knew her name, and unconsciously Jenna knew it would come to her, but for now Jenna was watching the woman hand over an envelope to the young man who put it in his pocket and walked in a purposeful way to the car park.

Jenna got up from her seat and walked towards the woman. As she got closer she realised it was Mrs. Davis who used to run the Scout programme with her husband. Mrs Davis was quite glued to her seat when Jenna approached her and said "Mrs Davis how lovely to see you. Was that your grandson you were just with?"

"Mrs Mitchell you are the last person I would expect to see here."

"Are you quite all right Mrs. Davis?" Jenna asked observing her strained expression.

"Never better and I am late for something. Good day to you." Mrs Davis said as she abruptly stood and began walking away. Jenna watched her leave and thought how strange.

Once Mrs Davis was out of Jenna's line of sight Jenna decided to do another walk around the garden before heading back to her parked car and making her way home, and in what seemed like no time at all Jenna was making her way to her car when she looked over and saw Mrs. Davis sitting in her car.

That's odd Jenna thought Mrs. Davis should have been long gone by now and with this thought in mind Jenna made her way over to her car and gently knocked on the passenger's door. Mrs. Davis looked up and unlocked the door. Jenna climbed in.

"Mrs. Davis are you all right?"

"Yes I will be. I owe you an apology. Mrs. Mitchell isn't it?"

"Jenna."

"I quite seem to forget myself these days. There is so much going on with the house needing repairs done and the cost of it, and then there's the new medication and I get all a dither as my mother would say."

"Is there anything I can do for you?" Jenna asked.

"No not really. I came back to the car and thought you can add being rude to people to your list and I was actually sitting here summoning up the courage to find you and apologise, but I became transfixed, so thank you for coming over. How are you coping?"

"Me. Well life has been eventful and interesting but I am trying to make the best of it." Jenna said with a smile.

"You should bottle that and sell it. I would be in to that." Mrs. Davis said and Jenna saw the Mrs. Davis of long ago make a brief appearance. They talked for a while longer before going their separate ways, and even though Jenna was pleased Mrs. Davis was more relaxed when she drove off with a wave, Jenna had a growing sense of disquiet which she could not quite stave off.

When Jenna got home she phoned Anne and invited herself over for a coffee.

"Come in Jenna" Anne called out when Jenna knocked on the door "its open." Jenna walked in and made her way to the kitchen. "Here is your coffee I thought you might enjoy it in the lounge."

"The lounge goodness me." Jenna said with a smile and Anne laughed. "I know we usually sit at the small table next to the kitchen but I have decided to start using the lounge again, the view of the farm and the trees is quite restful I find these days."

"You have changed the furniture around."

"Well you know what they say. A change is as good as a rest."

"Are you okay Anne?"

"Yes. Yes I am. Do you know I have had the best two weeks for a long time? Thank you for inviting yourself over, you are so busy that I feel as if I am intruding somehow when I get a spur of the moment urge to pop in."

"Well firstly I am very pleased you get spur of the moment urges, I sadly seem to get them less often these days than I used to, and secondly you are never intruding. I love the time we spend together." Jenna said.

"So when are you off?" Anne asked.

"In a couple of weeks for a few days. Sydney. Just some book signings and then I will be home again."

"So you will have to delay seeing Jean then?" Anne asked.

"Well Jean is not healing up that quickly so I think the timing will end up working out well. I have decided to drive down in another month. I needed the time to collect myself really and she understands that. When I do go I will be only gone a week. I think a week is long enough for her and me right now. Over summer I may stay longer, well that is the plan but that won't be until mid to late January and that is a long way off yet."

"So tell me what prompted you to call me if it isn't to do with your Sydney trip then?"

"I saw Mrs Davis at the gardens. Do you know her?"

"Mrs. Davis. The Scout Leaders wife?"

"Yes Anne the Scout Leaders wife. Do you know I don't even know her first name?"

"That makes two of us. He was very high up in the Scouting organisation here and nationally. Lots of articles about them in the paper. He did all the talking of course but she was always by his side and looking happy. They came into scouting quite late. Yes it was when they had the boys with them."

"Yes I saw her with her grandson she was handing him an envelope, and he just walked away from her quite quickly,

no purposefully like he was on an errand
or something, and I went over and spoke
to her and she was quite out of sorts and
left, so I did another walk around the
garden and went to the car and here she
was sitting in her car so I went over and
knocked on the window and she let me in.
She seemed quite agitated about
something. She's having repairs done
apparently and other bits and pieces."

"Grandson? No that can't be right."

"Well he looked old enough to be her
grandson."

"Jenna they had no children. They
had fostered two boys who were both in
Scouts and that is how they became
involved in scouting themselves. Yes it
was very sad. You weren't living here
then. You must have read about it in the
regional paper. Yes let me think now. It
was the youngest boy Darren. He had
finished his apprenticeship and just
turned twenty one when he began feeling
unwell and was told by his boss to man-
up, a term that is used far too much if you
ask me and no good ever comes of it. He
was a builder and they were very busy
with a new sub-division build from
memory and he collapsed at work. They

did tests and things and he died just six weeks later. Aggressive form of Pancreatic Cancer I think, and then just over one year later his brother Andrew was killed in a Forestry accident. Neither of the boys had children so there is no way Mrs. Davis will have been talking to her grandson."

"Oh" Jenna said "I see. Well given the circumstances I can understand why she didn't correct me then, but I wonder who he is? I haven't seen him before."

"Jenna please. When do you have time to take notice of people these days? When you are here you are usually focused on other things. Don't worry I am just envious of your life. Now while you are here let's choose our next movie and dining place shall we?" Anne said with enthusiasm.

"Yes I feel like watching the comedy we both commented on last week, is that on offer for a couple of ladies at the moment?"

"I will just get the paper." Anne said reaching down to the magazine rack "that British comedy at the local theatre is playing on Wednesday night."

"Local theatre it is then, how about I book us into the Indian restaurant for dinner. Dinner will be my treat this week.”

"There is no need for that." Jenna.

"I know but please let me do it just this once. Are you up for some ethnic cuisine?"

"I certainly am and it will match the movie perfectly."

With that sorted and the coffees well and truly finished Jenna left Anne to continue on with her day and Jenna went home to do some writing.

CHAPTER SEVEN

Jenna had been back from Sydney for several weeks and was packing for her break with Jean, who was recovering, and now finally out of plaster and walking with the aid of a walking stick. Her neighbours had been a great help to her, but they had the opportunity to go on a cruise and had phoned Jenna asking if there was any way she could come down before summer.

Jenna had of course consulted the Hat in the matter and he was as helpful as ever, but it did feel as though it was the right thing to do, so Jenna rang Jean, and after the pleasantries had been exchanged asked "Now Jean you don't have to agree.

I am just wondering if you are up for a visit in the next little while."

"Oh Jenna your timing is perfect. Cyril and Joy are going away on a cruise. Could you manage to come down in two weeks' time for a couple or three weeks?"

"Well I was thinking a week but if the Hat doesn't object yes I think I can manage that" Jenna had told her and left Jean to inform Cyril and Joy, which she knew she would be doing very shortly if she hadn't picked up the phone already.

That had been two weeks ago and they had flown by very quickly indeed. As always when Jenna was going away she took her perishables over to Anne and gave Anne her key and when she walked over she passed a car leaving Anne's driveway. Jenna made her way to the front door to find a distressed looking Anne there to greet her.

"It is only for a couple maybe three weeks and I am coming back." Jenna said light heartedly handing Anne the bag of perishables. 'Who was that?" Jenna asked.

"A very nasty piece of work who tried to hustle me into having work I do not need done and being very pushy about it. I am so glad you are here Jenna. I

have taken his number plate down and his
name. Please come in.”

"Give me the bag back and you sit
down. Do you want me to ring someone
for you? The Police?”

"No. I will be all right. Maybe I just
over reacted. He was so forceful and
adamant.”

"What work did he say you needed
doing?”

"The roof. He said the roof needed
repairing.”

"I see. I think a cup of tea is in
order and I will phone someone to come
and have a look at your roof, the chap who
did the work on Jean's place. He is honest.
What do you think?”

"Thank you Jenna but a cup of tea
won't do it. There is something stronger in
the back of the pantry. Second shelf
behind the tins of Spaghetti.”

"Well I must say I am surprised it is
very early, and I thought you put all the
alcohol down the sink.”

"I put most of it down the sink.”

"The Brandy or the Rum?”

"Brandy. Just a small one. And I
will have the cup of tea as well. I'm sorry
Jenna I am holding you up.”

"You are doing no such thing. Here is your Brandy I think you should sip it, the jug is on, teapot, teabags, cups and the phone book, phone." Jenna said as she made sure she was covering everything and within an hour the builder with a roofer he regularly worked alongside had been, checked the roof and was saying "Young chap? Calling at eight thirty in the morning he is keen I will give him that."

"Yes." Jenna and Anne said at the same time.

"If he comes back Anne you are to tell him there is nothing wrong with your roof or better still don't answer the door to him at all. There is a slight crack where we installed the new garage door for you, and I will send young Tony along to repair that free of charge."

"Thank you so much. I feel better already."

"Actually if he comes back take his details and call the Police."

"I already have his details. I wrote his number plate on the back of a piece of card."

"Good keep them handy. I'll get Tony to phone you before he comes to sort out a time with you."

"Thank you, and you too Jenna." Anne said.

"No need. Now I must be off. You have Jean's number if you need to talk and if I head away now I will be right on schedule." I can't help but think I have seen that young man before. Jenna thought as she was walking home. Once inside she walked by the hat and said "It will come to me. " And went to her bedroom to put the last of her items into her suitcase, closed it up and went to her car where she placed it in the boot. Her handbag was on the kitchen bench where Jenna headed to, making herself a thermos flask of coffee to take with her, which she put in her travel bag next to the sandwiches she had made earlier and some fruit.

Taking a deep breath and looking around her home she unplugged the jug. Did her final check of windows closed, doors locked, oven turned off, and proceeded to her car where she sat the travel bag on the floor in front of the passenger's seat placing it in the plastic box Jenna had purchased for that very purpose! Using the garage door opener to open the door, Jenna started her car and drove out onto her driveway closing the garage door behind her as she set off to Jean's, the plan being she would be there in time for afternoon tea. With a stop for lunch that gave her a good five and a half hours plenty of time all going well.

Jenna was well into her trip when she pulled over into a rest area where there were other people. Jenna was a great believer in safety first, and it never hurt to have some pleasant conversation if people were so inclined either she thought as she took her small collapsible table and chair out of her boot and set them up on a flat piece of ground. Taking her travel bag from the front seat she proceeded to pour herself a hot coffee and unwrap her sandwiches, which she ate with enthusiasm.

A couple in a camper van a little further along were stretching their legs and walked up to Jenna.

"Excuse me, I can see you are having your lunch, but I wonder if you would be so kind as to settle a dispute for us?"

"Well I'm not sure if I will be able to, but ask away." Jenna replied taking into account the Texan accent of the gentlemen standing in front of her.

"My wife Penelope insists you are the writer Jenna Mitchell."

"Oh I see. Well."

"Penelope here thinks that because this is such a small country she will see a writer amongst the common people."

"Oh yes I see."

"Well I am sorry for disturbing your lunch. Are you happy now Penelope? Interrupting this nice lady's lunch?"

"May I ask if there was a wager on the answer?"

"A wager. Why would I validate the notion with a wager?" The Texan said.

"Perhaps because you had a fifty percent chance of winning? Which I am sorry to inform you, you would not have done. I am Jenna Mitchell and it is very nice to meet you Penelope. Now perhaps you can tell me how you came to recognise me."

"I read your books. Oh Duane it is her I told you."

"And how did you come across my books?"

"Well I was in an airport stranded
and a kiwi lady was next to me also
stranded, we were headed in completely
different directions, and it was just so
random you could say, the whole thing,
and anyway when her flight was called she
handed me the book she had finished
reading and said this will help you pass
the time you will get to meet people, and
see a place new to you, and have a
pleasant read while you are at it, and I
was left holding the book. So that is how it
started really me reading your books.
They are great. You are still writing aren't
you?"

"Yes but less often these days. I'm
sorry I can't offer you both a seat. There is
a spare seat in the boot of my car if you
would like to sit Penelope? I am hoping it
won't take your Duane here very long to
apologise to you."

"Well I'll be." Duane said. "I get to
meet a published Author on a lay bye.
Wait till I tell Matt and the boys at the gun
club about this. You got this one right
Penelope. Good spotting my girl." Duane
said which led to smiles all around.

Some twenty minutes passed by
quickly, with talking and a book presented

for Jenna to sign. One of Jenna's earlier books as it happened, and it was a given that Penelope would have the proof of her meeting to show her friends back home. A rather lovely interlude as it turned out, with the couple giving Jenna their details if she was ever to make her way to Texas.

"Now Mrs. Mitchell you are welcome. I mean that. Most welcome. We have plenty of space and putting you up would be no bother at all." Duane said.

"Travel safe." Penelope said as Jenna started putting her things back in the car. Duane assisted with the table and chair. "You too." Jenna said, "And enjoy your stay with us." Jenna put the details they had given her and recommenced her journey.

Jenna arrived in Jean's driveway five minutes early to a waiting and smiling Jean. Jenna had no sooner stepped out of the car when she felt Jean's arms around her. "Welcome Jenna oh I have so been looking forward to this. Now what can I carry in for you?" Jean said having already opened the back door.

"Nothing I just have the one suitcase. Well perhaps you could take my travel and handbag. I didn't bring any food for you I thought we could go shopping after a cuppa?"

"No need I have plenty here, but if we want treats we could choose those together. As for the cuppa the jug is on and should be coming to the boil as we speak. Follow me in I have your room all ready."

"I thought you were using a stick." Jenna said.

"I am but I thought if I was trying to use a stick and carry something at the same time I might end up in a predicament again, and well frankly I am not up for another round just yet." Jean said.

"Or you could have let me make two or more trips to bring my stuff in."

"Yes well that just wasn't going to happen. You've had a long drive. Time to put your feet up." Jean said.

"I have been sitting for hours."

"Let's not argue. Sitting is hardly the same as driving." Jean stated and they both burst out laughing at the absurdity of it.

"I have missed you." Jenna said.

"Ditto. Now that everything is in your room I will make the tea and you can unpack now or later. Up to you." Jean said leaving Jenna by the wardrobe.

Jenna sat on the edge of the bed and took her mobile phone out of her bag and sent a text to Anne to let her know she had arrived safely and that she would tell her about her interesting encounter at the rest area when she returned home. She received an instantaneous reply "Only you could make me wait. I am making a note of it Jenna I am intrigued. Enjoy your time with Jean. Glad you had a good trip."

Jenna also sent a text to David so he knew she had travelled safely. Even though her family lived in other countries they still wanted contact with her when she set off on her trips here and there.

"Have you let David know you are here? You can use my phone if you haven't."

"Yes I sent him a text just now. I feel as though they don't trust me getting around on my own but then it is my own fault, after all I made them contact me when they were going from A to B." Jenna said.

"Nothing like karma is there?" Jean said handing Jenna a cup of tea and a rather delicious looking white chocolate and raspberry muffin.

"Thank you Jean I am glad we have started the way we intend to carry on. Indulgence all the way I see." Jenna said and they settled into their chairs, with conversation flowing easily between them.

CHAPTER EIGHT

Jenna and Jean were both pleasantly surprised by the fine days they were blessed with given that September had arrived and was historically a wet month. The weather was quite mild as well which made for working in the garden and going for walks very congenial. Jean was definitely making progress with her mobility. The Physiotherapy had strengthened her injured leg and she was walking without her stick more often than not now.

They had done planned day trips together, watched movies, gone to neighbouring shopping centres and townships, walked local beaches and parks, eaten well, talked up a storm and had a truly relaxing time together. But as with all things the time was nearing for them to go their separate ways again, and it was with a sense of sadness that Jenna packed her things ready for the drive home after having spent three weeks with Jean.

A knock on her bedroom door interrupted Jenna's thoughts. Jenna opened the door and Jean stood in the hallway looking quite sad herself.

"Do you need a hand with anything Jenna?"

"Well I was just going to bring my travel bag down for the morning so I can fill my Thermos up."

"Let me take that for you. I am just popping out for a moment." Jean said.

"Do you want me to drive you?" Jenna asked.

"No that won't be necessary." Jean said and with that both she and the travel bag were no longer in view.

Jenna heard a car, and a car door closing and then the front door opening. Jenna who was curious by nature made her way along the hallway to the dining room where sitting on the table was a Chilli-Bag.

"I couldn't resist. Our last night together for a while and I thought what will we have for dinner and I remembered Sam from along the road goes to Napier every week and brings a meal from Roast Hut for his tea so I left out my Chilli-Bag for him this morning and voila. Roast Hut just like the old days." Jean said with a smile and they both relished every mouthful.

Jenna headed off after breakfast the following morning, and allowed for the road works that had been in the local paper, which would add a good twenty minutes or so to her journey. Seeing Jean waving her off had a very bitter sweet moment about it. Not unlike the bitter sweet memories of the Roast Hut meals over the years.

Cyril and Joy Fellowes were due home in a couple of days-time so Jean would have a couple of days to catch up on things that are invariably left when you are entertaining visitors and having full days of fun and relaxation.

Jenna had made good time home and had decided she would unpack her things before going into town to get a few groceries. A quick walk around her property confirmed that nothing seemed to have changed much while she was away, apart from the weeds which always made an appearance with monotonous regularity whether you were there or not. Deciding on dinner Jenna hoped that the salads would look enticing in the Deli cabinet at her local supermarket, when her thoughts were interrupted by the phone ringing. Jenna answered the phone to a rather upset Anne "Thank God your home. Can you come over Jenna?" And with that the phone was dead.

Jenna walked briskly to Anne's and was confronted by a car she had seen before, leaving the driveway at speed, and as she got nearer to the house she saw a big mess on Anne's driveway, and looking up she saw a gap where there had been a perfectly good section of roof.

"Oh Jenna." Anne said tears flooding down her face.

"What on earth has happened?" Jenna asked trying to take the scene in.

"That young man. He came and just started ripping the roof off, saying I had ordered the work to be done. I have rung the Police and he was swearing and took off. I am sorry Jenna you have just got back and"

"And here comes the Police my word they aren't mucking around." Jenna said. "Hand me your phone I will ring our trusted Builder to get this secured for you. You talk to Sergeant Denton."

"Mrs Brown, Mrs Mitchell what do we have here?"

Jenna made her phone call, and Anne took Sergeant Denton inside.

"I can assure you there is a corner of the roof missing, and here I was thinking nothing much had happened while I was away. On your way home. Thank you. Yes I will tell Anne you will be here shortly." Jenna said before ending the call knowing at least the roof would be taken care of, but walking into the house Jenna wasn't so sure about Anne.

"Is there somewhere you can stay for a few days?" Sergeant Denton asked Anne.

"I don't want to leave the house." Anne said "I mean something else could happen."

"Anne you can stay with me." Jenna "It will be for a short time. Just until the roof is secured. I can hear a truck must be Paul our Builder, he did say he would call in on his way home." Jenna said rising to meet him, and following Anne outside they all were interested in what Paul had to say. Sergeant Denton began by asking "Anne has told me you had checked the roof and at that time there was nothing wrong with it."

"That is correct. It was actually Simon who checked the roof. I told her to make it quite clear to the young man that no work was needed. Sadly the status of that has now changed. I have got the young lads meeting me here, they will cover the roof I will contact Simon and get him to come and do the repair. When did this happen?"

"Sometime today. I was out and when I got back I saw the car on the drive and the mess and when I asked Sam the young man who was here what was going on he told me I had agreed to him fixing this corner of the roof. Which I hadn't. I told him to leave. Then I went inside and phoned the Police and then Jenna.   He started swearing, demanding payment, then got in the car saying "you'll be sorry I can tell you that" and then he took off down the driveway nearly running Jenna over as she was walking up, and then Sergeant Denton arrived."

"You know I have seen that car before. Just as I was leaving for my break with Jean. That car was turning into Maggie Dawson's place. You know I am sure I have seen that young man before. He looks very similar to. Oh yes the young man Mrs. Davis gave the envelope to in the gardens. You remember Anne I told you about that. I thought he was her grandson."

"Now you come to mention it."

"You say you saw a car similar going into Maggie Dawson's?" Jenna nodded and Sergeant Denton continued by saying

"Perhaps I will have a word with her and see if it is the same chap."

A good thirty minutes later Anne was in Jenna's lounge with her bag and toiletries in one of Jenna's spare rooms, there was a tarpaulin secured over her now damaged roof and a rather unsettled, apprehensive vibe was in the air.

"Jenna do you think Insurance will cover the damage."

"I don't know Anne but we will contact the Insurance Company in the morning. They will advise you on what needs to happen, but I am thinking you will need to lay charges with the Police for wilful damage?"

"Oh yes Sergeant Denton did mention that and a few other things. Perhaps I should talk to him before I contact the Insurance Company. What were you going to have for dinner?" Anne asked.

"Salads. I was going to go the Deli bar at the Supermarket. How about we go together. You can choose whatever you like." Jenna said and picked up her purse.

The supermarket was very busy and the two women were making their way to the Delicatessen Bar when Willow Gibb a fellow parishioner came up to them.

"Anne, Jenna, good to see you. I haven't been out as much of late. How are things with you?" and before either of them had a chance to answer her question Willow continued with barely a micro-pause "before you say anything please know I have learned my lesson. I am so embarrassed. I can't tell you. My family far from being understanding are understandably furious with me, but at the end of the day it is, no was my money, well technically, my husband's, our money and the family money inherited of course but my money now and I." Willow stumbled over her words with great aplomb.

"Willow it is lovely to see you too." Jenna said "I have been away and Anne is in a little adventure of her own right now. Not of her own making of course. Now what is all this about you being embarrassed."

"The work on my house, which I paid for and didn't need doing." Willow said. "Well it was put to me that it needed to be done of course, and any delay would make things much worse." Willow told them.

"And who was it that told you this?" Anne asked her.

"Well Sam. Sam Black. I thought everybody knew."

"Willow what does this, your Mr. Sam Black look like."

"Well he is young. Very confident. Has brown hair. Drives a"

"Maroon four door car and demands to be paid in cash?" Anne asked before Willow had time to finish asking the original question.

"Well yes. How did you know that?"

"Willow have you been to the Police about this?" Jenna asked.

"The Police. No. Why ever would I go to the Police? It has been bad enough dealing with my family and they have gone to the bank over the cash advances I took with my Credit Card."

"What was the nature of the work this Sam did for you?" Jenna asked.

"Well he said I had a huge issue with my roof and by the time he got to the bottom of it my roof was coming off and he presented me the bill for that day's work and said he needed the money paid there and then. The Bank was closed so I used my credit card to get the money out for him and he set about fixing the roof for me, on a pay as you go basis."

"Did you ask him to fix the roof?" Jenna asked.

"Well of course not. I had no idea there was anything wrong with the roof until I found him on my driveway saying his inspection had highlighted a problem which would need to be addressed urgently."

"So how did he get access to your roof?"

"Well he said he had been asked to do checks in the area and..."

"Willow have you eaten?" Jenna asked.

"Not yet." Willow said looking quite confused at the turn the conversation had taken.

"Well we haven't either. May I suggest you and Anne choose your salads and whatever meat you like, I will have Kumara Salad it is a personal favourite and perhaps some Champagne Ham four slices please, and I will just make a call while you are doing that, and come back to you shortly. Order what you like it is on me." And with that Jenna stepped away from them and called Sergeant Denton who confirmed he had not dined either and would meet them at Jenna's in around twenty minutes.

With dinner on the table and everyone having a bit of everything a rather impromptu meal with eclectic ingredients was on offer with a fourth dinner guest eating heartily indeed. "So Mrs. Gibb you had no idea that other people were being subjected to impromptu roof inspections?"

"Well no. I don't get out as much these days and when I am out I am rather keen to get back home again. And please call me Willow. Mrs. Gibb seems so formal. I haven't been formal since I left work." Willow stated.

"Well Willow I would like you to come to the Police Station in the morning and fill out a statement on what has occurred. If you can remember the dates that would be useful."

"The dates. Well they won't be a problem I wrote everything down in my diary." Willow said between mouthfuls. "Excellent." Sergeant Denton said and smiled.

CHAPTER NINE

The Police Station became quite busy with people making statements and apart from Anne, Bridie, and Willow there were many other residents who had been caught out by urgent building repairs ranging from roofs, to pavements. It seemed no part of a property was immune from needing attention and repair when Jayden Parks, Pete White and Sam Black came calling in the Maroon sedan. They were it transpired the same person, with the same modus operandi. To fleece people of money for work that was never needed to begin with.

Jenna was quite shocked at how widespread the entrepreneurial skills of this one individual had spread in such a short space of time, and even worse than that the absolute lack of anything substantial being done to show for the money he had extracted or extorted from his unsuspecting, far too trustful customer base.

For Sergeant Denton as the facts came in, an all too familiar picture emerged, with gambling being at the very centre of that picture and a few other activities around the edges. The case was handed onto a team of worthy investigators and all those affected were assured of their day in court which in actuality never happened, because Jayden Parks pleaded guilty to receive a diminished sentence.

"You know Jenna there is a book in here." Tania said in one of her catch up phone calls.

"There may well be, but I have no intention of writing it. You have investigative reporters who would do a fantastic job of writing a book on this subject.”

“But they were all older residents.”

“Yes Tania most of them were, but not all of them. I write for and to bring pleasure. If I write at all.” Jenna said.

“Apart from the last two books which both resonated with your readers and were non-fiction, and this subject would do extremely well. It has everything to sell.”

“Yes Judy. Shall I call you Judy from now on?” Jenna said.

“I get why Judy did what Judy did now I am in the big chair, but I am not Judy. The thing is Jenna you were right there when it all happened and did its big reveal for the want of putting your perspective into context.”

“Tania I do not have a perspective other than I am grateful I didn’t arrive home to find my roof on my driveway. This was a conman going about extorting money pure and simple. A young, well buffed, personable man, up to no good, and with determination and stealth who nearly got away with it.”

“Exactly my point. I couldn’t have written a better introduction myself.”

"You are incorrigible." Jenna said.

"I prefer the word hopeful. How are they by the way? Your friends."

"That is the other side of something like this. They are going to take a while to come to terms with it all. There has been some real damage amongst families over it all. Now that we have turned the conversation to family how is yours?" Jenna asked.

"Very clever how you do that. You are quite skilled at changing direction I will acknowledge that." Tania said with a laugh and their conversation continued on the personal rather than the professional relationship they both shared.

Jenna also caught up with Jean by phone and arranged to meet Pamela Tiggs from the Coffin Club for coffee later that afternoon.

"You know Jenna we have missed you. Well to be fair I have missed you. I appreciate the donation you made but it is you, and your input that I have missed to be more precise." Pamela said over their coffee meeting.

"Yes. I had intended to come back as usual but when I did come back there were new faces, and I was grieving myself.

Letting the children go to Vincent and Bridgette had more of an impact than I had anticipated. I had gone from full on to nothing, and I didn't handle that at all well." Jenna said feeling appreciated and embarrassed at the same time.

"Jenna would you be up to discussing some plans to move us forward. You won't have to come to the club, just a meeting or two, just the two of us and maybe a couple more people?"

"What have you in mind?"

"We have been approached by young people with terminal illnesses and asked if there is a place for them."

"And you said death doesn't have an age barrier I hope." Jenna blurted out.

"Exactly the conversation that needs to happen and I can't think of a better person to get the message out. What the young people are telling me is that their parents are focusing on keeping them supported and alive for as long as possible, while they themselves are wanting to have some control over their end game."

"Tell me Pam. How have we come to this? This people dying longer stage."

"It is your book that has opened this discussion. They want to meet you. The young people. Would you be available to talk with them and listen to what they are proposing?"

"That depends. What are they proposing?" Jenna asked.

"A collaboration. Young with old, old with young, a passage through an ending."

"So you have read my book."

"More than one. Jenna you have made death a wonderful part of life for people." Pamela said.

"And when would this meeting with a couple of people take place?" Jenna asked.

"We are free Saturday afternoon." Pamela said.

"This Saturday?" Jenna asked.

"Whatever Saturday you can make it." Pamela said.

"Next Saturday then, two o'clock. Knowing young people they will want to add to their proposal knowing they have an audience. My experience of young people is they can be very specific." Jenna said smiling at Pamela.

"Thank you Jenna." Pamela said and they looked at each other knowing that another successful journey together had begun.

Jenna was feeling very blessed the following Saturday afternoon, as she sat with four young people who eloquently introduced themselves, and then using technology launched into a power point presentation that any sales magnate would be impressed with. So comprehensive was their argument that Jenna and Pam sat looking at each other without the need to say anything at all. This completely disarmed the four young presenters.

Shontelle a very attractive, slim, brunette stated 'So you like everyone else think we are being too negative, too proactive?"

"Well I can't speak for Pam." Jenna said "But I think if we can organise some funding it is an excellent idea. Perhaps we could get the local art class involved at the polytechnic, and ask them if they would be willing to put some design concepts in a folder to give young people ideas on what their coffin artwork might be. I only bring this up because apart from that and the actual money you seem to have covered everything else."

"You are not put off then?" Gary asked tenuously.

"If I had been put off I would not have involved Mrs. Mitchell." Pam said. "The thing about our Mrs. Mitchell is things happen when she is in the picture and I think approaching the design school is an excellent idea."

"Well I wouldn't know how to go about doing that." Fergus said.

"Me either." Jenna said "so I will make some calls and find out. And as we are going to be in a working partnership arrangement it is Jenna. Mrs. Mitchell seems far too formal." She said with a smile and winked at Pam.

"Well I have your contact details." Pam said, "So I will be in touch and we will go from there."

And one month later they had not only gone from there, they were all entering a world where they had never travelled before. The design world had opened up a whole new perspective on time, art, cost and materials that could be used rather than the coffin being painted, which appealed to young people very much. Yes even in death technology was having a role to play and Jenna found that oddly comforting, she also realised there was a place for a book for teens dealing with imminent loss in and of their lives.

Knowing how Tania would put a time line on a writing project Jenna decided to work with the young people to add their perspective on the 'Dying Longer' reality and what that meant in real terms for them and their families.

The young people arranged interviews with Jenna, at the hospice, hospital, in private homes, and the park. Jenna took her recorder along and analysed hours of conversation to compile the similarities, solutions, feelings of self and others, frustration, anger the whole gamut of human emotion when faced with an inevitability of huge proportions and the subsequent denials and acceptance that join and affect people involved on the journey.

It was with great sadness that within six weeks of their very first meeting Anna passed away. They had worked with a small team from the polytechnic art design class on her art work and stencils had been made up for them to use to paint her coffin.

Both Jenna and Pam had been surprised by this, believing that Anna the most technologically savvy of the group would choose a printed option to be overlaid on her coffin, but as she said "This is something I want an organic feel to. Me doing something for me. No contracting it out to others."

This group of now three worked in shifts, tirelessly together with Pam's support and Jenna's frequent food parcels, and older members of the coffin club to complete the project.

At Anna's funeral Jenna spoke to acknowledge the wonderful support Anna had received from family and friends as she prepared for her final departure.

The coffin was typically Anna. Exquisite design with a simplicity of colour used that made one feel both impressed and comfortable at the same time. Of the four young people Anna was the quieter, and most organised. Many tears were shed as the coffin was being readied, and unknown to Anna her parents had asked if they could see what it looked like before her passing in case they needed to replace it on the day, but Pam had explained that Anna was pouring her heart and her thanks for all the support she had received over her lifetime and knew it would be perfect. "May even surprise some people. Mum and Dad will love it." Anna had said.

Anna's father had said almost that when he gave his eulogy. "We have been blessed with independent thinkers, and Anna reminded me of that when I went down the track of disapproval where death and preparing for it at such a young age was concerned. In her quietly determined way she said "Dad you have taught all of us to take ownership and responsibility for the decisions we make, why do you think I would abdicate my responsibility in this?" As tears fell from his puffy eyes he continued by saying. "You and Mum have raised us well. Be proud. That is not the conversation you think you will have with any of your children, but there it is. Anna you were, are loved and you were right about your coffin, there is no way we would have replaced it, it was as Pam said a surprise."

Anna was carried by her three brothers and Gary with her parents following her to the hearse, and a private burial service was held after refreshments. Pam and Jenna were invited to attend along with some of Anna's close friends and the family, and at Anna's request the design team.

Jenna had attended many funerals over the years and none of them were happy occasions, but this one was memorable, and parts of it would live on. Jenna had decided that the cover page of her book would bear the artwork of the coffin, and reveal the actual coffin at the end of the book with a tribute to the four young people who had put the coffin project for their age group and circumstances together.

A surprise phone call from Penelope and Duane Chambers in Texas on her return home was just the tonic she needed.

"Thought we would call how did the event go?" Duane asked.

"Event is not what Anna would have called it, but it has gone and now we must all go on without her."

"What you have done Jenna. You and Pam together. Humbling." Duane said.

"On the same note," Penelope added "How's the book coming along?"

"Making progress." Jenna answered her.

"What has Tania said about it?" Penelope asked.

"That is a conversation I will have with her next week when the final draft is ready, a living testament to Anna who said to me one day."

"Instead of waiting for her to give you a deadline just do a draft and hand it over. You don't have to wait to be dying to surprise people."

"Rather profound and sobering for one so young at the time, but I have managed to get it to the draft stage. The addition of quotes from the interviews has helped with that, and everyone involved wanted Anna to see how it was shaping up. She did quite a bit of the proof reading for me so it is our book really. Why are you asking about the book?" Jenna said.

"Well we thought we might order a copy or two. See if it is up to scratch." Duane said quite sternly.

"I thought you didn't read my books." Jenna stated.

"Not your fiction but I have read the other two and I have expectations for this one."

"Of course you do." Jenna said.

"We both do." Penelope added 'But as you can tell I am hanging out in anticipation, and he as always has expectations." To which they all laughed.

Putting the handset back onto its cradle Jenna smiled at what an unlikely encounter and meeting with them had been, and even more unlikely their keeping in touch with her. It was then that Jenna realised that Duane was a bombastic buffoon with a very big heart. How thoughtful of them to phone her today and as she put that thought to one side the phone rang again.

"Jenna it is Jean. How are you? And don't tell me you are fine."

"I am sad Jean. Very sad."

"As you should be. My thoughts and prayers are with you. Now put your feet up, you have had a long day." Jean said before ending her call, and as Jenna was walking over to her chair there was a knock on the front door. Jenna opened the door and there was a delivery man with a huge bouquet of flowers standing there.

"Jenna Mitchell?" He asked.

"Yes I am Jenna Mitchell." She answered.

"These are for you then." He said with a smile.

Jenna took the flowers inside and placed them on her dining room table, and took the card out of the envelope which had been carefully placed in the flowers.

"Your welcome. No need to call. Now put your feet up. Love Jean xx"

Jenna began sobbing and looked over at the picture of the four young people from their first meeting, not wanting to think about how long the other three would be here.

CHAPTER TEN

Life continued in a slow rhythm for Jenna. Her latest book was getting the final edit. Meetings with Tania were going well. Gary, Shontelle and Fergus had completed their coffins and all had decided to include their families in the project. As expected they were all in varying stages of palliative care, and also as expected they were helping others on their journey as well.

Being proactive they had a committee of young people to carry on with the Coffin Club long after they had gone, and the older members of the Club were in awe and admiration of them.

Pam still as involved as ever had organised with Tania a supply of Jenna's books on death, preparing for it, and living on from it. The books were ordered by young and old alike. For Jenna, she found this quite cathartic, but helping people was at the core of her writing these books so she was pleased her words were informing people again.

Over coffee with her neighbour Anne, Jenna reflected on how her words had gone from educating and informing people when she wrote her recipe book series, and then entertained people with her fiction books, and now she was educating and informing people while entertaining her readers now.

"You know Anne I rather think I have gone full circle with my writing."

"I'm sure you have Jenna, but just think of all the people you have helped and entertained over the years. More than you know I can guarantee that. Has anyone ever researched how many people actually read the purchased book?"

"Very possibly, and if no one has I don't intend to be the one who does that." Jenna said with a smile.

"Have you thought anymore about your Texas invitation?" Anne asked.

"Yes I have given it much thought and Tania of course thinks it is a great idea. Her suggestion was I accept after for the launch of the new book."

"Of course she did. Quite a focused publisher she is these days." Anne said.

"You have no idea." Jenna replied "But I am still thinking about it. Duane means well, but I really don't know how I would go over there. I mean compared to here it is so big."

"Jenna Mitchell who are you kidding. You have travelled extensively. What is your problem?"

"I stay with Family or in a Hotel room with my own company, or with Jean."

"Oh so you are scared? Of what a loud Texan or the culture change."

"You know I have no idea, and when you say it like that it sounds like I am being very silly."

"You think!" Anne said. "Now onto our movie this week. What do we feel like watching?"

"An action." Jenna said.

"Really? Well okay then an action it is." Anne agreed and went to get the paper.

The regular movie and dinner evenings were very enjoyable Anne and Jenna were saying over their dinner at the local Thai restaurant. "You know" Anne said, "We should have done this a long time ago. It is so easy to be insular when one is in a marriage isn't it?" Anne asked.

Jenna was looking at her and could see Anne was waiting for a response, "You know I have never thought about it quite like that. In our marriage we seemed to have the compartmentalized thing working very well. Too well as it turned out because as you and most other people now know Adam had two lives going on and neither side knew of the other. Insular? Well one can be loyal to a fault maybe. Insular? Interesting word, but then it all depends on how one looks at their life isn't it? I mean you say insular someone else could see devoted or grieving, or obsessed. It rather depends on where you are and where your marriage is, in that moment isn't it?"

"And so says the writer, but to be fair I hadn't thought of it in quite those terms."

"Hindsight is a great tool people often say as you know, but I think beating yourself up or trying to justify actions after the fact is a plague on people. We can speculate all we like after the fact, the fact is we make decisions in real time. We don't think about things like are we being insular, over the top or anything else. We arc just too busy doing. Are you going to do the dessert tonight Anne?"

"Yes I am. Fried Banana for me with ice cream. And you?"

"I'm full thanks I will pass."

"No surprise there." Anne said with a knowing smile.

Once home Jenna made herself a warm milk drink, and sat with her feet up holding her cup with both hands to allow the drink to warm them up. Oh the quiet Jenna thought. Just bliss. Sipping her drink she thought about what Anne had said, and reflected on how insular her life was becoming before Cyril Fellowes had phoned about her spending time with

Jean. Yes thought Jenna it is a slippery slope. An easy path to walk along and be snared by the convenience of not having to engage with people. Perhaps all the happenings in recent times had meant that she, Jenna Mitchell had dodged a bullet all be it a rubber bullet. Back to making lists to keep myself busy and engaged with people Jenna thought as she got up from her chair and walked over to the kitchen sink depositing her now empty cup there, and washing it, before drying it and putting it back into the cupboard in its space. Yes everything in its place Jenna thought, before retiring to her bedroom for a good night's sleep.

The morning brought heavy rain and even heavier winds. Jenna heard a large cracking sound as she was eating her breakfast cereal and knew that the snap, crackle, pop, was not coming from her bowl of Rice Bubbles. Getting up from the table and going to the back porch where her outdoor shoes were sitting on the shoe rack, she put them on and did a walk around her section. At the side of the front garden furthest from the front door she saw her old gum tree minus two large branches and cracked down the middle.

"Jenna. Jenna get inside. You will catch your death." Anne called out as she walked purposefully towards the back door, joined soon after by Jenna.

"What on earth are you doing out in this?" Jenna asked Anne.

"I heard an almighty crack and came straight over. I wanted to make sure you were all right."

"Thank you Anne. I am fine. But you shouldn't be out in this weather."

"No one should, but at least I thought to put a raincoat and hat on. Two items you seem to be missing and you are drenched."

"Oh. Well I did get my shoes on." Jenna said with a smile.

"Not funny." Anne said. "Would you like me to phone Mr. Morris, he has always done our trees and done a good job to."

"Thank you yes I have used him before for someone he is very reliable. I will just get changed." Jenna said and having done so joined Anne in the dining room and finished eating her breakfast. Anne had made coffee and they waited together for the heavy rain to subside before Anne made her way home.

It was later that afternoon that Mr. Morris arrived to take a look at the tree and his verdict was as Jenna had expected. Too much damage to salvage the tree so he would be back to cut it down. In the meantime he cut the fallen branches into more manageable lengths, then took them away, vowing to come back with some assistants to take down the tree and take the stump out.

Jenna was extremely grateful that the tree was quite a distance from the house, and had told Mr. Morris just that. Mr. Morris was extremely grateful on Jenna's behalf that the tree had cracked in the direction it had, as even though it was a distance from the house, being a very large tree, it would have landed on the house in any case. The branches had fallen away to the left and had done some minimal damage to the border gardens but that was easily fixed. Mr Morris knew that when people were building houses, and doing landscaping they really needed to factor these things in. Established trees are wonderful, but where they are is important. Of course Mr. Morris did not say any of that to Jenna. Jenna was not the one who planted the tress, or did the original landscaping. He would discuss with her the health of a couple of her other more established trees as they in his opinion needed to be removed as well, before they suffered a similar fate, however with ten more people to see, and debris to clean up that was best left for another time.

Jenna decided to use the wet weather as motivation to do a stock take of her pantry. Many things had shifted with her and checking best before and use by dates had been brought to her attention on a consumer programme earlier that month, when she made a mental note 'I had better chuck my stuff out'. So Jenna decided today was the day as soon as she had phoned Anne to give her an update on the fate of the tree.

As Jenna had suspected many things in her pantry were no longer 'safe' so there were quite a few gaps on the shelves when Jenna had removed items that had been there way too long. Jenna had those items on the dining table and was making a list of them. What occurred to Jenna at the conclusion of this exercise was what she had in the pantry. Stuff that she had bought that Adam liked. Not only had it been sitting in the pantry for that long which was quite an embarrassment in itself, but more pointedly, Jenna conceded she had never enjoyed the food that those ingredients had in them, and never really thought about it.

Jenna did the cull of the list and took all the things she didn't use or like off it and determined to purchase more Jenna appropriate items from now on and perhaps not stock the pantry quite so well, to negate the need for this exercise to happen again. Smiling at her accomplishment Jenna put the items into a plastic tub and disposed of the contents into the rubbish and the packaging into the recycling bin, thinking I will not be that wasteful again. This was more of a statement than an admonishment and perhaps another part of letting go in the grieving process?

Jenna thought about this and realised that apart from photos kept for her children and grandchildren this house had hardly any remnants of her life with Adam in it, and yet it was still a home.

All the shifts, all the dramas, all the change, and Jenna was still in a home and making the best of her life and helping others.

Jenna smiled and made a call "I have special coffee. If I put my hat and coat on can I bring it over and use your water to make us both a cup?"

"Absolutely." Anne said "I will put the jug on and I may even run to a piece of shortbread."

No sooner had Jenna put the phone down and gone to the pantry to retrieve the sachets of special coffee she had found behind some items in the pantry than the phone rang. Picking the handset up from its cradle an excited male voice was talking very quickly and Jenna found herself asking "Who am I talking to?"

"It's David. I just had to ring you. I couldn't wait. They have offered me a partnership in the business here. What do you think about that? Deanna, Rich and Steph are all wrapped."

"So it's Rich now?" Jenna asked "I think it is fantastic. Congratulations." Jenna said and at the conclusion of the conversation realised that the chances now of Richard and Deanna returning to live in New Zealand were very remote indeed.

Picking up the sachets of coffee Jenna made her way over to Anne's with good news to impart. Jenna was very proud of David and he was deserving of this acknowledgment. Yes a good day all around, even the tree was to be removed and Jenna thought she would get Mr. Morris to check a few of the older trees as well, better to be safe than sorry were Jenna's thoughts as she knocked on Anne's door.

"Sorry I got a phone call just as I was picking up the coffee. A phone call with great news imparted. Let me tell you all about it." Jenna said and Anne smiled.

"You know the coffee always tastes better when good news is attached. The water is ready." Anne said.

CHAPTER ELEVEN

Jenna felt blessed with good news. David had been offered his partnership, Vincent, Brittany and the children were doing very well, as was Karla and Bryce, and there were new arrivals pending for the family. Yes life was very good Jenna thought as she walked around her refreshed garden. Old trees had been removed and new ones planted in safer growing areas from the house to allow for their expansion. Flower beds and shrubs had been planted in the gaps and the whole section seemed lighter and brighter too.

Quite uncharacteristically for Jenna she decided to purchase a return ticket to see Karla and Bryce and be there hopefully to welcome their first born into the world. Yes I will surprise them she thought, and phoned her travel agent as soon as she got inside to make an appointment to see them. Things came together rather more quickly than Jenna had imagined but by four o'clock that afternoon Jenna was back home with her tickets in hand, travel insurance arranged and a shuttle van to take her to the airport to be organised.

The list was made and things were being methodically ticked off. The shuttle was ordered by five o'clock and Jenna was having a pre-dinner coffee with Anne to inform her of her travel plans.

"I must say Jenna I thought you would be going to Texas. Duane and Penelope have asked you more than once."

"I know they have and I am considering it, but I feel Karla would like me to be there with them."

"Has Karla asked you to be there?"

"No Anne, but then to be fair she probably wouldn't. I mean. Well we don't seem to." Jenna found herself faltering so she simply said "I have decided I want to be there with them."

"Well that's okay then." Anne said. "Go and enjoy. I will keep an eye on things for you."

"Thank you." Jenna said, before their convivial conversation commenced in earnest and before they both knew it the dinner hour had been and gone, so Anne suggested cheese on toast and a cup of homemade soup together before Jenna went home.

"It has been a day." Jenna said as she left Anne's and made her way home.

The next morning Jenna had packed her suitcase and purchased some baby clothes she had previously ordered from one of her church group lady's and she was all set.

Knowing that Deanna was due to have their baby soon as well Jenna had decided to add a flight, and change a flight to see both her Australian families as she now thought of them. Why she hadn't done that in the first place she was unsure, but it would be all fixed up by the afternoon and then Jenna would have her new tickets and be packed ready to leave the following morning.

It was the usual ritual of Jenna taking the consumables over to Anne, and then Jenna returning home, walking around her property, and waiting for the shuttle. The shuttle arrived on time and Jenna was off. What Jenna didn't know was that the phone had begun ringing as she left the driveway.

Jenna checked her baggage in and got her boarding pass. Her phone was off and everything was in order. Her flight was called and Jenna boarded the plane feeling quite proud of herself.

On landing Jenna collected her bag, went through the arrivals process and turned on her phone as she walked to the taxi ramp. Jenna got into the taxi and while the driver was putting her suitcase in the boot she glanced at her phone and saw missed phone calls and text messages. Jenna was reading one of the text messages when she was asked "Where to madam?"

"The Maternity Hospital on…"

The driver finished the conversation with the name of the hospital to which Jenna said "Yes please."

On arrival Jenna with her luggage in hand made her way to the desk and asked for directions as to where her daughter was and found herself in a delivery room with some very surprised faces looking at her.

"I just checked my phone." She said as she put her luggage against the wall out of the way. "Felt I should be here."

"Another big push now Karla." The mid-wife said.

"She has been asking for you." Bryce said.

"Well here I am." Jenna said reaching over to squeeze his hand. "Come on Karla I would say you are nearly there."

"A really big push now" the midwife said and then there was a crying baby, father, mother and grandmother.

"Would dad like to cut the chord?" The midwife asked.

"I think we will let Nana Jen cut the chord, what do you say Karla?"

"Why don't you both do it? I can't believe you are here mum."

"Me either. I really thought I would be having a lovely cup of tea in your lounge and enjoying the surprised look on your faces. Best laid plans even impromptu ones can be altered."

"I was praying you would come. I started having trouble the day before yesterday."

"She wouldn't let me phone you then. Stubborn."

"Well let's all agree that Divine Intervention is a very reliable tool in situations like this and best of all I didn't have any worry on the way over. Everything has worked out perfectly. There you go little one." Jenna said as she put her hand over Bryce's when he cut the umbilical chord, and with that baby was given to a very tired, very relieved mother.

"Well done Karla." The mid-wife said.

"Thank you Rachael for all you have done. Rachael this is my mother. Jenna Mitchell."

"What a pleasure. Mum and I have read many of your books but the two non-fiction one's you have written on living longer and living on is it? Fantastic. Well I will let you have a moment. I will be back shortly." Rachael said and with that she left them alone.

"Even here they know you."

"I am sorry Karla. This is your moment. I would never take from that."

"Don't be silly mum. Rachael must have recognised you from your book covers. You are helping people. Something you have always done one way or another. Here she comes again I take it there will be more pushing now for the next bit."

"Do you have a name for him?"

"We thought Blake after Bryce's grandfather?"

"Blake. I like that. I think he will be a very handsome Blake." Jenna said and then the last of the birthing process was complete.

Bryce phoned David at home and told the family the good news that mother and baby were doing well, and that Nan Jen had arrived unexpectedly but at the perfect moment."

Jenna decided to tell them she had a ticket to come and visit them as well while she was over and Deanna said she would try and follow suit and have their baby early as well to which they all laughed.

Jenna and Bryce went home leaving Karla with Blake at the hospital while he was in neo-natal as a precaution. They were no sooner in the house with Jenna's luggage in the spare room than Jenna heard sobs coming from along the hallway.

"Bryce. Oh dear."

"We thought she was going to lose him. I thought not again. We are so close."

"Well he was just in a hurry to meet you. It happens. Now I think we both need a good stiff drink. Lead me to the drinks cabinet and have a seat."

"I am so pleased you are here."

"Me too. Now glasses."

"What am I thinking? You must be starved."

"I ate on the plane. Now here you are" Jenna said handing Bryce a generous scotch whiskey and holding a smaller one for herself "congratulations dad you've both done it."

"Well yes we have."

Jenna smiled and what a journey it had been for them she reflected.

Jenna was there when Karla and Blake arrived home and was able to help with the settling in process. Their fractured relationship seemed to have finally healed with the arrival of this precious son, and Jenna was very happy about that.

Leaving to go to spend time with David and Deanna was bittersweet as it turned out, and also timely. Deanna who had always carried well past her due dates went into labour a week early and Jenna was there for that arrival as well. So a grandson and a granddaughter. How truly blessed I am Jenna felt as a stray tear slid down her cheek.

"We thought we would name her Sarah" David said.

"Sarah. That's lovely."

"You were going to tell us you were coming weren't you?" Richard asked.

"No I wasn't and I was going to swear Karla and Bryce to secrecy but that all seemed futile on my arrival so Bryce decided to tell you."

"We love having you, but mum no more surprises. Let us all know okay?"

"Okay. You know Sarah your father has always been good at telling people off.

You will find this out for yourself in time of
that I have no doubt."

"Me either" said Richard.

"We girls don't get told off by dad
much Sarah so don't worry, but then
mum. Well mum makes up for that."
Steph said with a smile.

The time away went all too quickly
and Jenna was soon on a plane back
home. Her experiences though had been
good ones. A year full of children it had
turned out to be, and on her arrival home
Jenna had a message waiting for her from
Anne that Gary Phillips had passed away.

Jenna met Pam at the funeral and
they were both joined by Shontelle and
Fergus. Shontelle was more philosophical
about Gary's passing than Fergus. Fergus
took the view that his passing should have
occurred first. Whereas Shontelle said
quite simply "It is when your time is up
and clearly his time was. Was it a
surprise? Yes because the doctor's
expected him to live longer, is it a shock?
No because we know that Cancer or any
terminal illness can slow or accelerate
depending on any number of factors, and
Gary himself last week said I hope the
suffering for people outside of myself ends

swiftly as well when the time comes. It's like people know. If Gary was here he would tell you he had accepted that his time had been well used, and he would be right about that."

"How can you stand there and say that?" Fergus asked quite aggressively.

"Because he wrote it and wants you to let people know that at his funeral Fergus. Remember we all decided and agreed we would treat our passing as soldier's treat the inevitability of death as a cost of war. They have a letter for loved ones prepared and those letters are held in safe keeping until they are needed. I was given the letter so to speak and I will be handing it over to you."

"He was supposed to be reading out my letter." Fergus said as a tear slipped down his cheek.

"Well your letter is in a box that he gave me so you can decide who will read that out now."

"Perhaps we need to have a box for these letters and keep the box with Pam. From what I am hearing the delivery of the sentiments the person has left for family and friends is more important than the person who delivers it. You know in the

second world war, the Captains used to
write home to families when a soldier had
fallen, but there were so many, often they
would enlist the help of others to do the
writing and they would sign them off."
Jenna said.

"The original copy and paste."
Fergus said.

"Not quite." Pam said "But perhaps
it is something that can be discussed at
your next meeting. You have a good
committee now and they may have other
ideas you could consider."

"You see, even with his death Gary
is allowing us to make things better for
people." Shontelle said and burst into
tears. Fergus put his arm around her and
they walked away.

"I don't think I am up to attending
Gary's funeral Pam. It is getting very
hard."

"I know, I was thinking the same
thing myself, but then I look at what these
four young people have managed to pull
together, not just for their age group but
for older family members as well."

"Let me think on it." Jenna said
knowing that the coffin club was for the
living preparing for death, but the reality

was that those left behind needed the love around them to be freely given as they dealt with the finality of the coffin, and the occupant they once loved in it.

Looking across at Fergus and Shontelle Jenna also knew their time was coming to an end and they would expect her to be there for their families, so as hard as it was, and as much as it hurt, Jenna knew she would be there for Gary and his family as well.

That's the thing with projects. They start as one thing, grow and become bigger involving more people and you seem to be in the mix at all stages. Yes Jenna thought there is no point being superficial you are either all in or all out, and for now Jenna found herself all in.

Seeing that Pam had joined Shontelle and Fergus, Jenna made her way over to them.

"Jenna if you are finding these funerals a bit much we do understand. You could just come to the wake." Fergus said.

"What Fergus means is, you have faced a lot of loss recently yourself. We know it will be hard for you." Shontelle added.

"I will take it under advisement." Jenna said. "Now I must go. Pam if you could call me tomorrow."

"Yes of course." Pam said knowing that she would be picking Jenna up and they would both be paying their respects to the family and attending the funeral together.

On her arrival home Jenna made herself a coffee put her foot up and gave thanks for all she had, all her family, and her friends, and she also gave thanks for the blessing of being cared for by those around her. Yes even in a time of personal loss two young people thought about Jenna and the reality of her losses.

As Jenna retired to her bed and felt the softness of her pillow as she closed her eyes she fell asleep feeling very blessed indeed.

CHAPTER TWELVE

Jenna was very mindful of Christmas fast approaching, it was November already and she was more than busy enough. She had determined with her family that a monetary gift for a family outing of their choice would be their present this year and they were all discussing what they might do and when. Jenna thought it would be a simple solution for everyone. They would all get the same amount money from her and they could do what they wanted with it. The family however took it to a whole other level, they had decided to do the family outing on the same day, and share their outings in real time. Given time zones, countries and weather Jenna wasn't at all sure how that was going to work out, but then she didn't have to really. All Jenna had to do was hand over the money and let them enjoy it.

So November was here and Jenna was marvelling at the speed with which it had arrived and reflecting on the year to date and was lost in her thoughts when the familiar sound of a Skype call interrupted them. Going over to the computer and answering the call Jenna was surprised and thrilled to see Jason.

"I can see you are excited about something." Jenna said smiling as his mum Eden came into view as well.

"We are" said Eden.

"We have booked flights for you to spend Christmas with us this year, with an open return date. All paid for, our gift to you, and we thought that as you would be in the States you may be able to spend time with the Chambers." Jason said with a smile.

"What if I am spending time with my family?"

"You're not. I checked with them first."

"So they are in on it as well?"

"We wanted to surprise you."

"Well you have certainly surprised me, but"

"No buts," Eden interrupted "It is time Jenna for us to give back. We have a life here because of you. We both have a life here, a very successful life."

"Yes and I am pleased for you both, but you two have made that life. Each of you." Jenna said.

"And without the opportunity and support from you it wouldn't have happened quite like this now would it?" Jason asked.

"Well thank you. I will get in touch with the Chambers and see what dates they may be available. They will probably be traveling themselves or have you already contacted them?" Jenna asked.

"No we thought we would leave that up to you. I will send the tickets through to you when you have spoken to them. I bet you never thought this day would come." Jason said sounding very pleased with himself.

"Certainly not this quickly or out of the blue that's for sure. I hope you don't have any more surprises in store? This one is quite enough." Jenna said.

"We can't wait to see you. Do you want to go to Canada to see Vincent?"

"Oh no I don't think so we are spending next Christmas together, there have been developments there." Jenna said.

"Talk again soon." Jason said and the screen went blank.

Jenna looked through her contacts and immediately contacted the Chambers and Duane answered getting Jason's Skype address from her and saying "Penelope is going to be gob smacked. Of course we will have you. Leave it to me I will arrange everything. You don't have to give it another thought. I will be telling this Jason boy he has made my day."

"He is a young man Duane, and to be honest I am still taking it in."

"You will be enjoying his company and ours soon enough. People love you Jenna because you have a love for people.

You put the good out, so enjoy the good that comes back to you."

"I don't expect good to come back to me." Jenna said.

"Lucky some of us put it out there for you then. I can't wait to tell Penny. I will Skype Jason now." And with that he was gone, and Jenna felt like she was on a roller coaster, not that she ever intended to be on a roller coaster. No that would never be on a bucket list that Jenna wrote never, but a phone call to Jean at four o'clock was quite on the cards.

Jean by the end of their four o'clock conversation seemed more excited than Jenna about the impending trips and Jenna was beginning to wonder what she had agreed to by saying yes to visiting Texas but already those flights had been booked and there had been very ebullient emails sent through with those details as well. Penny it would seem still hadn't arrived home and Jenna was starting to have a stomach full of butterflies, which by six o'clock she had tried to quell with dinner, but to no avail, so she decided the next course of action would be engrossing herself in a book, this too fell short of the desired effect so Jenna found one of her favourite DVDs and enjoyed two solid hours of escapism with a hot chocolate break in the middle. Her butterflies now settling, she made her way to bed, and as she passed the hat she said "an interesting day, not that it seems to have affected you."

The following morning brought a different set of circumstances entirely to her home. Jenna was washing up her breakfast dishes when she was interrupted by a knock on her back door. She made her way along the hallway to answer the door and was greeted with Anne standing there obviously in pain with a tea towel wrapped around her wrist.

"Can you take me to the hospital Jenna? I came to the back door so I could get straight into your car."

"Would you rather I take you to your Doctor?" Jenna asked.

"They are so busy I won't get in." Anne replied her eyes beginning to tear up.

"Make your way to the car and I will meet you there in a moment." Jenna said going to get her car keys, and check the front door was locked and the stove turned off. Picking up her phone she dialled the Doctor and explained the situation, then went to the back door locked that, unlocked the car and opened the garage door, as she sat next to Anne, and helped her with her seat belt before seeing to her own.

"The Doctor will see you as soon as we get there." Jenna told her and was answered with a nod.

On their arrival at the Doctor's Anne was seen very promptly and they were sent to the hospital. The fact that Anne had broken her wrist was obvious once the tea towel had been removed, the only question that remained now was how many bones were broken in her wrist.

It was a sombre trip over indeed, but once there Jenna found a car park and was able to make her way to the Emergency Department where she had dropped Anne off and they were reunited once again. X-Rays revealed surgery would be needed and Jenna had no time at all to be concerned about her upcoming trip.

Anne was admitted and surgery was scheduled for early that afternoon. Anne told Jenna to go home but Jenna decided to stay by Anne's side until after the operation was done and Anne was out of recovery and on the ward.

When that time did arrive it was seven o'clock that evening and Anne who was talking cheerily was quite done in. "You know Jenna I feel as though I have just run a marathon."

"Well serve you right for not training properly first." Jenna replied and they both laughed. Jenna left the hospital at eight o'clock and decided to phone in the morning to check on Anne's progress. As she was driving home she came across a detour due to an accident and found herself on a road she was not that familiar with. She had been on the road before, many years ago when it was farmland, cattle, dairy cows, and sheep dotted the landscape then and there were pine trees, pockets of them she remembered, but now not a pine tree or animal in sight. Plenty of houses, street lights and a small shopping centre with a takeaway outlet clearly visible with its large illuminated sign. Jenna indicated and pulling off the road and into the car park she found an empty space right near the entrance way. She walked in an ordered a cheeseburger and some fries. I am in training for my trip she thought and smiled as she sat down at a nearby table.

Anne was discharged the next day with a follow up treatment plan in place and a promise from Jenna that she would be caring for Anne for at least the next forty eight hours, which in actuality became a week, by mutual agreement.

Over dinner on the last night of that week Jenna brought Anne up to speed with the final arrangements of her impending trip.

"What will your kids say to that?" Anne asked "
You are missing another Christmas with them."

"I have been over recently and they are fine with it. Apparently Jason had run it by them first and I wouldn't be at all surprised if I get to see Vincent and family while I am there, even though I have said we are spending next Christmas together.

"How long will you be away for?" Anne asked.

"It looks like about two weeks, but as we know things can change."

"Oh my how you are changing Jenna Mitchell you used to have a plan for everything."

"Yes and then life started interrupting my plans big time, so I have learned from that. Sometimes you need to be accepting, breathe and let the plans go to engage with the life, even if it has a cost at times. It all seems to work out in the end." Jenna said philosophically.

"You know Jenna if you hadn't shifted to this house I would not have coped nearly as well as I have. You Jenna Mitchell are a healer of damaged people?

"I don't think so." Jenna said quite taken aback.

"You don't have to think anything about it." Anne said "I am telling you, you are. People are always better after you have been involved somehow. You seem to have a knack for it, and a knack for joining dots together. Living next door to you has added a very good vibe to my driveway, and I am letting you know now that when you are away on these trips, excursions, promotions, whatever form they take, you are missed and not just by me I will have you know. You make a positive difference wherever you go Jenna.

If you could bottle that you would be a very rich woman indeed."

"I think Anne the anaesthetic is having a residual effect. Perhaps you should stay another day or two?"

"You know a flaw you have is taking a compliment." Anne said kindly.

"I have many more as well." Jenna said and winked at Anne.

With Anne now in her own home once again Jenna was able to re-engage with her routine such as it was, and life settled into a familiar pattern for her once again.

Surprisingly Jenna felt content rather than complacent, and also fulfilled. "I am blessed" she said to the trees and the shrubs as she was weeding one mild Tuesday afternoon and the birds chimed in as if to agree.

At the supermarket the following day Jenna found herself standing next to Sally from the council. "Hello Sally."

"Hello Mrs. Mitchell how are you?"

"Well and you? Is that an engagement ring?" she asked and Sally's smile answered that question. "I am so pleased for you."

"Not anywhere near as pleased as my mum. I think she thought I would never get a proposal." Sally said with a laugh, got her items from the delicatessen and moved off. While Jenna was waiting for her salad and cold meat she felt very happy for Sally, and a very warm feeling encompassed her.

CHAPTER THIRTEEN

All the travel arrangements had
been made and Jenna was going to be
away for quite a length of time. What she
had thought would be two weeks had
become six weeks, and Duane had been
quite insistent that her stay with them
was not only going to be at least a month
but eventful, interesting, relaxing, and a
whole ball of fun. Jenna being quite the
conservative wasn't going to ask what the
fun component entailed, but she did feel

that Duane and Penelope had arranged something. Jenna had no proof of this of course just a feeling, and the older Jenna got the more she trusted her feelings.

The weather was warming up and the days were getting longer which made for great growing conditions in the garden. Anne was healing up well and the weekly movie and dinner were back on the agenda. On the odd occasion there wasn't a suitable movie they agreed on, they got a DVD out instead. An upside down night as Anne would say with the dinner first then the DVD rather than the normal early movie followed by dinner before going home.

Phone calls with Jean continued on a regular basis as well, and Jean divulged she was treating herself to a holiday in the South Island with her friends the Fellowes. Jean had never been to the South Island so she was quite excited about seeing different scenery, and visiting different places. She had purchased a digital camera and was attending lessons at the local Community Centre once a week learning how to use it.

Jenna smiled as she thought about how Jean's life had changed significantly

over recent years. It was almost as if a
new Jean was emerging from the shadows
of the lives she had lived before. "You are
not one to scoff Jenna Mitchell." She
chided herself as she began sorting
vegetables for her dinner "You too have
had several reincarnations over your life
time all be it due to changing
circumstances if I may be permitted to say
so." She said to the carrot now in her
hand awaiting the peeling process,
justifying her personal situation.

And peeling and slicing or dicing the
vegetables Jenna realised that it is
actually the same for everyone. Often
your circumstances dictate the tenor or
tenure of one's life. Not always but
mostly. Jenna had started writing to
increase the money she needed for her
family, then money came more easily, not
just because Jenna had a back stop but
perhaps because Jenna expected more
money so it turned up. These days Jenna
had abundance beyond anything she had
ever dreamed of on the financial front, but
that money had not come to her by the
means she had envisaged at all, and it had
arrived at a cost other than hard work and
long hours.

Jenna also had taken it upon herself to ease the load of others and give still others a hand up, and now Jenna was in the privileged situation of being able to do what she wanted, when she wanted, and how often she wanted, with ease, but people kept giving to her. What a dilemma to find one's self in Jenna mused as she placed the now prepared vegetables into her steamer and turned it on. The chicken was roasting nicely in the oven and its aroma filled the room with the expectation of visitors arriving. Jenna turned her attention to the salad next and set about making that, and putting the salad dressing in a small serving jug.

With the food sorted the setting of the table came next. Jenna couldn't actually remember how long it had been since she had prepared a meal for someone other than herself with all the trimmings. Yes there was even going to be dessert. Pavlova with fresh fruit salad, and whipped cream all prepared earlier, waiting for their debut moment. The cheese platter could wait until later Jenna decided and busied herself with the nibbles. She had literally just changed into her good clothes as her mother would call them when there was a knock on the door.

Opening the door with a beaming smile she said "Welcome, how lovely to see you to her first guest who was swiftly followed by the other invited guests and what a mix of people Jenna had in her family room and then around her dinner table."

Jenna had invited Mr. Benton her solicitor, Pam from the coffin club, Anne her neighbour, the new Minister or Reverend as some people called him Mr. Fisher and his wife Elizabeth known as Betsy, Dallas Robinson the funeral director, Tania her publisher with her husband Sebastian known as Baz. What a fantastic mix of people they were, the night went by far too quickly, with all the food eaten, with liquid refreshments to accompany them, with the coffee and hot chocolate complimenting the cheese platter concluding the meal was an unexpected delight. So relieved was Jenna that someone was better at the coffee than she, that Jenna felt compelled to do a speech to acknowledge Dallas and his Barista skills.

After they had all left Jenna determined she would host an evening like this again which was a mute-point as the group had decided they would have turns hosting an evening for everyone themselves. Dallas had announced he was willing to do up a roster so this could be an ongoing event and perhaps each person could take a plate. There were lots of laughs about this given his profession "no brains allowed." Baz said.

"Yes" replied Dallas "My father warned me about those types of comments." He said with smile.

As Jenna laid her head on her pillow she smiled and reflected on how life was to be lived and realised that whatever fun Duane had planned she would not only go along with it, but make the very best of it.

Jenna felt lighter that night than she had felt for a very long time, almost as if a fog had lifted from her, and she slept soundly.

Rising to the sound of the Tui's in her large trees Jenna donning her slippers and dressing gown made her way outside via the back door to hear their birdsong unfiltered by brick and insulation and what a treat. It was a very brisk but sunny morning and the borders were erupting on a daily basis adding different shades of yellow, pink, and reds in the garden and what a picture they were. The daffodils and tulips were in their last stages now and with the new flowers putting on their show an explosion of many colours was really coming into its own. Yes new beginnings and the wonder of natural celebration was there for all to see. Blossoms on the trees, Roses coming into full bloom. Yes Jenna decided there and then that she would phone Anne and after breakfast see if Anne was free to join her on an excursion to the Hamilton Botanical Gardens, with perhaps a flask of coffee and a sandwich?

On this thought Jenna headed to the bathroom and washed her face. A morning ritual instilled in her by her mother. "Make sure to wash your eyes properly I don't want to see any sleepy dust at my breakfast table." She would say and with a gruffness that always surprised Jenna. One day she remembered asking her father "Why does mum wake up so grumpy?" "Wake up grumpy," he replied with a wink. "Lucky you don't hear her when she puts her head on the pillow at the end of the day."

Jenna picked up Anne at ten o'clock that morning and they set off for a walk around the gardens and have a bite of lunch together. Well that was the original plan, but as it happened their plans changed, and being a pair of ladies who were open to embracing change in its many forms, they ended up going to a large shopping complex to browse, then bought tickets to a movie that was opening that day, and then they decided to stop and have dinner at a Thai restaurant before ending their very full very unscheduled, unplanned day with a hot chocolate each. Very racy indeed.

"Do you know Jenna I am absolutely filled with Joy and exhausted all at the same time?"

"Yes Anne I know what you mean. It is absolutely years since I have had a day unfold like this one, and what a gem it has been. Thank you for coming. You know I do think it is more about the company sometimes. I remember years ago having planned to do something with Jean and we both looked forward to it very much and it was a play. Yes a play by the local theatre group and it turned out to be a disaster. Poor things. Nothing seemed to go right. Curtain changes went awry. The cast forgot lines. The prompt seemed to be completely overworked for one part of an act if I recall correctly, and oh yes at the intermission there was all this clapping outside. That's right it was the cast applauding the prompt for saving the day. At the end of the show when the cast came out to take a bow I remember they moved the prompt forward and introduced her to the audience thanking her for saving the day. Very dramatic and theatrical, and the great thing was the audience who gave a rapturous applause for her efforts."

"Do you know Jenna I am always amazed at what you remember, and how it appears at the perfect time. Dare I ask did you go back to theatre after that?"

"Oh yes. Jean often went to the theatre and would invite me along on occasion."

"You still miss her." Anne said.

"Do you know Anne I do miss her, but at the same time I am happy for her, although I can't tell you how she made a new life for herself, and yet we still keep in touch. I'm thinking of inviting her up for a couple of weeks in the autumn. Jean loves the autumn here."

"I don't know Jean very well. We have met a few times of course, but I was wondering if she would be up for a short cruise to the islands, and if you would consider availing yourself of that opportunity as well."

"Are you restless again Anne?"

"No not restless, but I do enjoy a cruise and I think you would like them, and I see no harm in asking Jean to join, and if you decided not to come perhaps it will be Jean and I having fun."

"I believe they call that hedging your bets. If you want someone you know to go with you that's fine. You have mentioned these cruises to me before. It's not that I don't want to go, it is more that I don't see myself sitting around all day doing nothing."

"Jenna I have been on several cruises now and I can assure you, you can be as lazy, or as rested as you like, but you can also be as busy as you like."

"Let me check my schedule and I will ask Jean if she is interested as well."

"If you used the experience as research for a book it could even be tax deductible for you." Anne said with mischievous smile.

"To quote a line from the movie Jerry Maguire with Tom Cruise starring 'You had me at' in this case you did have me at short cruise." Jenna said with a smile.

"They have plugs for laptops too if you wanted to do some actual writing." Anne said as she stood up from the table.

"Now you are being facetious." Jenna said.

"I should know better than to even try to win a round with you on words. Thank you for today Jenna. I woke up this morning looking at another rather unfilled prospect of a day, and your phone call changed all that."

"For both of us Anne. I thought two or three hours, and here we are just making our way home and it is nearing my bedtime. I will give Jean a ring in the morning about the Cruise and let you know what she says. Now to the car and home. Lead on Anne I will get this."

"There's no need Jenna."

"For years I wanted to be able to treat myself and others and I love doing it. It brings me immeasurable joy." Jenna said.

"Okay then. Thank you. I will just visit the ladies room while you take care of the bill and next time it is my shout. I like doing things for others too. You don't have a monopoly on that Jenna." Anne said as she left Jenna who rose from the table and made her way to the counter to settle the bill.

CHAPTER FOURTEEN

Jenna phoned Jean the following morning as she said she would, to find the answer phone the only respondent on duty so Jenna left a message and putting the hand piece in its cradle on the conclusion of the call and got on with her day.

Jenna was cleaning her kitchen cupboard, well in truth rearranging her kitchen cupboard when the phone rang.

Picking up the handset which she had placed on the kitchen sink bench she answered by saying, "Hello Jenna speaking."

"I am hoping it is you Jenna otherwise I have rung the wrong number again, and that is something that seems to be happening to me on a regular basis these days." Jena said.

"You should get Cyril to programme my number into your phone that way you will get me every time."

"And is that how you do it?" Jean asked. "Be honest."

"Well no but I do have that function and I have used it, and it is handy especially when one is tired or under stress."

"So that is code for it is set up but I dial the old fashioned way from memory of numbers."

"Most of the time, yes." Jenna conceded.

"Well as your reward for being honest I would like to accept the offer of going on the cruise and ask if Joy can come too."

"What about Cyril, I mean they do everything together don't they?"

"Yes most of the time but as it happens Cyril will be away for a month

around that time with his War Veteran
trip. It is an annual thing, but next year it
is a Centenary and they are staying away
longer. I think he goes once every three
years normally, but they have all made an
exception for this next one. Do you think
Jean would mind?"

"Well I don't know but I shouldn't
think so. Let me give her a quick ring and
I will get back to you." Jenna said ending
that call, and immediately phoning Anne
who said she would phone Jean herself
and let her know the more the merrier.

So Jenna thought as she returned to
her kitchen cupboard next year will be the
seasons of travel by the looks of things,
and before she could get too carried away
there was a knock on her front door.

Jenna stopped what she was doing
and went to the door, opening it she found
she was looking at a man she didn't know
and found herself saying "I am not
interested in buying anything today, or
signing up to anything today."

"Well that is a relief." He said. "You
don't know me. My name is Bryce Waters
and I am hoping you are Mrs. Jenna
Mitchell?"

"Yes I am."

"Well Mrs. Mitchell I am hoping you can help me re-home something that I found in the house you and Adam Mitchell lived in for many years. I do have my Driver's License if you want to note down some details."

"Please Mr. Waters come in. I have my phone at the ready if things go awry."

"You talk like you write. My wife is quite an avid fan of your books as it happens."

"So Mr. Waters if she is an avid fan how do you know how I write?"

"Yes, well I may have read a couple of her books." He said with a smile. "The reason I am here is because we have been refitting the kitchen and I found something and wondered if you might know who it belongs to? Have you ever lost anything in the house? Anything of sentimental value perhaps?"

"Sentimental value, well the only thing I can think of is my great Grandmother's paste engagement ring. I remember putting it on in the morning. It had been a day I felt like dressing up. Silly really. The kids were playing and I felt so dreary. It's the ring I would wear on special occasions, and then later in the day I noticed it wasn't on my finger and I couldn't find it anywhere. I actually thought our daughter had hidden it. I looked for months but never found it."

"Could you be a little more specific?"

"Of course the ring has three rather large paste stones clear like diamonds, and a thick gold band, and oh yes a small circle of gold with a whole in it on each side of the stones."

"Well in that case I think this may be yours?"

Mr. Waters took out of his jacket pocket a small Jewellery box, opened it and revealed "My great grandmother's engagement ring. Oh my!" Jenna exclaimed as a tear inexplicably escaped from her right eye. "I'm sorry where did you say you found it?" Jenna asked trying to gather her composure.

"Behind the stainless steel top of the kitchen sink unit, directly under the window."

"The window. Yes I must have put it on the windowsill. I did that you know took my rings off before I started the dishes. Then I decided to use gloves so the rings stayed on, but that was some time later. I'm rambling. I am sorry. It is

just such a shock, well a pleasant
surprise. ”

"So I can see it is definitely yours
then." He said with a smile "Can we agree
it is completely unexpected?"

"Yes we can certainly do that.
Thank you so much. I know it only fake
paste I believe, but she wore it religiously
apparently. Treated it as if it was really
worth something. Well clearly it was
worth a great deal to her. Well in those
days once you were 'spoken for' engaged
you needed to show that to people didn't
you? Ward off other suitors so to speak so
it was a big deal. Now days of course
there are man-made or computer or is it
industrially made stones which look like
the real thing. Some stones have even
more brilliance to them than the real thing
and the colours are so crisp."

"Mrs. Mitchell."

"Jenna please."

"Jenna these are actual stones.
Diamonds. Old diamonds to be exact.
You will need to get this ring insured. I
have the valuation for you." Mr. Waters
said handing Jenna a piece of paper.

"Forty thousand dollars that can't
be right."

"As I said large, old, diamonds. Quite the collector's item if you were to sell. I am a Jeweller Jenna and we bought the house for our son who has been away overseas and is due to come back. We are doing the house up for him. I knew as soon as I saw it glistening that I needed to return this ring to its rightful owner and that it was the real deal. Did you ever claim insurance for it?"

"No. No as I said I thought it was a paste ring."

"Well then it is yours to enjoy once again."

"I don't think I could wear it now, not if it is worth that much."

"Get it insured and give it many outings. Jewellery is meant to adorn, not just appreciate as my father would say."

"A cup of tea or coffee perhaps? Jenna said remembering her manners.

"That would be lovely, and if it is not too much of an inconvenience could you sign a book for my wife?   Presumptuous I know but..."

"I would be delighted." Jenna said and went to the kitchen to fill jug as Mr. Waters went to the car to get a book for Jenna to sign.

As soon as Mr. Waters left Jenna couldn't help herself. She took the ring out of the jewellery box and put it on her finger and incredibly after all those years it sat perfectly and shined wonderfully and Jenna felt oddly complete, as if a missing piece of her had returned. How odd she thought looking at the ring on her finger which felt the same, sparkled more but apart from that looked the same and to think it was worth so much money, but as Jenna reflected had she known it was so valuable the ring may never have been worn. Jenna realised that for all the years her great grandmother had been maligned and treated like a fantasist she had indeed been telling the truth, and it was in the opinion of others that the ring had remained safe, because they chose to believe it was worth nothing in monetary terms. A free insurance policy one might say. Insurance Jenna thought yes she would make a call right away and then maybe take Mr. Waters advice and wear the ring again.

Jenna having made the call to her insurance company had got her ring added to her policy. She was advised not to take the ring overseas, and to have it housed in a secure place when she wasn't wearing it, but apart from that they were happy for her. Jenna of course didn't tell them the back story, just that she had inherited a ring valued at forty thousand dollars and it had arrived with the valuation, which she was directed to send them and she did.

With her computer at the ready Jenna scanned the document straight away to the email address given, and the photo of the ring that Mr. Waters had also given her, and within no time at all the whole process was complete.

No sooner had Jenna concluded her phone call with the Insurance Company, than it rang again.

"Hello did I forget to do something?" Jenna said as she assumed it was the young man from the Insurance Company ringing to get some more information.

"I don't think so," Anne said "I haven't asked you to do anything yet, but I was just about to. Would you mind coming over and giving me a hand to pull one of my shrubs out. It is looking very sad."

"I will do better than that," Jenna said "I will bring tools with me to make it easier for the both of us. See you in a jiffy." Jenna said as she put the phone down.

See you in a jiffy Anne thought I haven't heard that expression in years.

Jenna locked the front door and made her way to the garage where she kept her gardening and other tools. David had told her to get rid of them, and give them to him, but Jenna had resisted that request. Her parents always had tools. "You never know when they may be needed" her father had said one day. "You may not need to use them yourself, but someone else may need to use them if you ask them to do something for you. These are practical things Jenna you need to be aware of. People always want to take what you have. They see their need a priority over yours, but imagine if they shift away and take your tools with them, and then you need to use those tools for something and you don't have them. What then?"

"Buy new ones? Borrow someone else's?" Jenna had answered him thinking the question had been directed to her and at nine years old she felt very important to have been asked.

"No Jenna. The whole point I am telling you this is so that you know once you own something it is yours and you must be responsible with and for it. Maintain it. Care for it. Keep it."

"Like my bike?"

"Yes Jenna exactly like your bike."

"But my bike is too small and my knees hit the handle bars already. Am I never going to get a bigger bike?" Jenna had asked.

"Replacing something is not the same as giving it away." Her father had said rather more sternly than he had intended and seeing the frown on his face Jenna skedaddled out of there.

Arriving at Anne's prepared with her gardening gloves on and gardening tools in hand Jenna made her way to the back door where Anne was waiting.

"Thank you Jenna. It is over here. I could have called the gardener, but I thought surely I could do it myself and then."

"Let me guess," Jenna said "by the way you are walking gravity turned up as you were pulling on the shrub in an effort to get it out and gravity won?"

"With mother nature rebuking me at the same time." Anne replied. "I thought if we both pulled together." Anne began saying before Jenna interrupted her.

"I know you have one good hand available but really. What were you thinking? You do know don't you that there is no achievement award for stupidity? We are supposed to learn from our mistakes." Jenna said and realised she sounded just like her father had when she had made what she thought at the time to be a sensible enquiry about her bike situation. "Fortunately Jason showed me how to remove a shrub more safely."

"May I venture to ask if you have had gravity with Mother Nature issues of your own?" Anne asked.

"You may ask me whatever you like, but I have managed to gain knowledge from a myriad of experiences and I make better decisions as a result. Sadly not all the time, but then I am human and as we know humans are fallible across many areas of their lives, and in many situations."

"So that would be a yes then? What can I do with my one good hand, given that it is my shrub?" Anne asked.

"Well given that I have the tools," Jenna said as she was cutting the branches off the shrub with her pruning saw, "picking up the branches I am cutting and stacking them somewhere would be a great start." Jenna said.

"I thought we would be cutting them to go into the rubbish tin." Anne said.

"In a bygone era maybe but not these days. No we will stack them up and tomorrow I will go down to the hardware store and buy a shredder, and we will use it to make mulch for your garden. How does that sound?"

"Jenna they are expensive aren't they? I can get the gardener to come and take it away."

"I need one for my place anyway. Now let me see. Yes." Jenna said looking at the bottom of the shrub "I think I will dig around this here, and here, and, Anne can you just steady the top for me while I," and with a great thrust on the spade in an upward motion the base of the shrub succumbed and rose up with roots intact freeing itself from its earthly home, and was carried by the women to be placed next to the branches.

Jenna returned to the now exposed home and rearranged the surrounding dirt to fill that hole in. Jenna then went over to the tap and washed her gardening tools and smiled unashamedly.

"You should be pleased with yourself." Anne said. "I will put the jug on for a cup of tea? Coffee?"

"Coffee please and I am smiling in remembrance of something my father said when I was nine. It has taken awhile but I get it now. He would be proud of me I think." Jenna said placing the tools by Anne's back door and removing her gardening gloves, taking her shoes off before making her way to the kitchen to the coffee that was made and waiting for her.

"Just how did you try to get that shrub out?"

"I tried to push it over with my foot."

"And let me guess. Your foot kept going."

No sooner had Jenna sat down with her cup of coffee and raised the mug to her lips saying "And going," and then exclaimed, "Jenna what on earth is that on your finger? I don't think I have seen it before?"

"Oh." Jenna said with delight "This is my great grandmother's engagement ring and it has come home to me."

"There is a story there I feel." Anne said, "Can you tell me about it?"

So Jenna did, and the rest of afternoon seemed to melt away.

CHAPTER FIFTEEN

It was while Jenna was purchasing the garden shredder that she determined she would make a donation to the local hospice. Jenna had been thinking about this for a while to be fair, and knowing she would be heading away overseas, she thought an early Christmas present to them and the Coffin Club would bring her some early Christmas joy. Her thoughts were interrupted by the now familiar voice of Craig the store attendant who was assisting Jenna to get the shredder into her car asked her to move a little to her right and push. Even with the back seats folded down, the shredder had literally just squeezed in. Jenna looked at her helper and he said "That last shove did it. I hope you have someone at your end to help you get it out."

Jenna looked up and addressed Pam who was approaching them. "Pam I wasn't expecting to see you here." Jenna said.

"Nor I you. I was going to phone you actually."

"Hold that thought for just a moment would you? I wonder when you are free could you pop around to my place?"

"Well as it happens I am free now and the timing couldn't be better. I think you may need a hand to get that out of your car." Pam said.

"Oh yes, and very possibly how to work it as well."

"That's easy. We have one of those. You won't have any problems at all. I can show you if you like?"

"That would be great. I have vegetation to shred at my neighbour's."

"Anne?"

"Yes. Well when you have the branches or whatever ready we can do it then."

"They were cut two days ago and stacked ready."

"Well today is the day then. I will see you in half an hour." Pam said and made her way to her car.

"Thank you Craig." Jenna said "As you can see I will be fine at the other end. That was a stroke of luck wasn't it?" Jenna said and Craig walked back to the store.

Jenna locked her car and made her way to the bakery to get some muffins. Pam loved muffins. Double chocolate chip were her favourites, and Jenna liked Raspberry with White Chocolate, and Anne? Now Jenna had an issue she had no idea what Anne liked when it came to muffins.

"How may I help?" The shop assistant asked.

"Two double chocolate with chocolate chip muffins, and two raspberry with white chocolate muffins please." Jenna responded knowing that someone would be enjoying two muffins.

The removal of the garden shredder from the car was as easy as it had been squeezing it into the car to begin with, but it was also as successful. Pam set about taking it from the box and flattening the cardboard putting that into the recycle bin as she went, and suggested they took it over to Anne's to begin the shredding straight away.

Jenna phoned Anne who agreed that would be fine and off they went. A bit like going for an impromptu walk around the block with the kids really, Jenna thought as they set off. Pam, Jenna, the muffins, and the shredder. Well at least she didn't have to buy an ice cream on the way home she mused as she quickened her step to keep up with Pam who seemed to be on a mission, or perhaps she was just a very fast walker.

With the shredding done and placed around the garden, the ladies had also enjoyed a cup of tea and a muffin together, and the shredder was wheeled to its new home by Pam who found the perfect place for it in the corner of the garage.

"Jenna I need to ask you something. You can say no."

"Before you do that I have something for you. Come with me. Have a seat, I will just be a moment." Jenna said as she walked through to her office.

"Sorry it took so long. Merry Christmas." Jenna said handing Pam an envelope. "You can open it now or later, up to you."

"It's a bit early for Christmas isn't it?" Pam asked as she opened the envelope and took the card out finding a cheque inside and looking at it. "Jenna this is way too much. Twenty thousand dollars. I was going to ask you if I could borrow two for a few families in need until I could get some more funding in then pay you back."

"Funny how things line up isn't it. A receipt is all I need in return. Even with the coffins being reasonably priced and people doing them themselves. I know what the real need is out there. I am not insulated in cotton wool Pam as you know."

"What will your family say?"

"My family are well provided for Pam, besides it is what I feel I need to do that is important, and I am more than happy to do this. I am going away for Christmas and I wanted you to be able to enjoy yours without having to worry about funds.”

Pam got up and hugged Jenna, walked to the front door and got into her car. She drove down the driveway and pulled over to the side of the road and burst into tears with a sense of relief that completely overwhelmed her, and a very grateful heart.

Jenna went into her lounge and sat down with her feet up and took the current novel she had been reading off her small table and began reading, she glanced across at the clock which told her it was five fifteen and she realised it was almost time to get her dinner ready. Determining to read to the end of the chapter she put her eyes and her mind on the book, and the next thing she knew it was very dark, the clock was chiming and she couldn’t see a thing. She reached over and put her table lamp on, and saw the novel on her lap, looked over to the clock and saw it was nine o’clock.

Jenna put the bookmark in the her novel and placed it on the table, then got up and went over to the hall light turned that on, then returned to the table lamp and turned that off. She checked the front door was locked and made her way to her bedroom passing the Hat and saying "Clearly we need an early night. See you in the morning." And with that Jenna walked to her bedroom turning her bedside lamp on there and stepping back into her hallway to turn her hallway light off at her bedroom end.

Changing into her nightgown and getting into bed Jenna remembered not a lot else until she was woken at nine o'clock the next morning by the phone ringing.

"Jenna. It is Tania and I have just received notification that you are up for an award. Well we are up for an award for the two non-fiction books and of course we are all very excited. Can you attend the dinner with us? I mean do you have anything planned this month, like trips or?"

"To be honest Tania I have just woken up and to answer your question no I have nothing planned until December the 20th. Can you email me the details and I will get back to you later today. Are you all right Tania you sound very?"

"Excited. I am so excited. This is the first time we have been nominated for anything since I took over as the Publisher. Emailing now." Tania said as the phone went click.

"Well I never." Jenna said and put her phone in its cradle on the bedside cabinet and rolled over falling asleep again without any effort whatsoever. Waking around lunchtime Jenna was surprised at how long she had slept and decided that a check-up with her Doctor was in order. She had been feeling quite tired recently but put this down to her being busy and getting older.

Jenna managed to get an appointment at three o'clock that afternoon due to a cancellation and by the time she had got herself showered, dressed, had something to eat, vacuumed the house and had a cup of coffee it was time to leave. The appointment took twenty minutes and Jenna seemed to have had every part of her scrutinized with a furrowed brow visible throughout the examination and interrogation process, and then Jenna was dispatched to the Laboratory for bloods to be taken.

Jenna arrived home at five o'clock and set about preparing her evening meal which to be fair was in the fridge ready to have someone do something with it from the day before. So Jenna mused as she ate her meal this is what it is like when you sleep most of the day away, your day is gone very quickly, and then Jenna remembered Tania had sent her an email, which she followed up by a return to her lounge chair, and the novel she had been reading the day before, reading it through to the end, before retiring to bed.

The weather was fining up with just the odd shower, which for spring was not unexpected. The temperatures were on the rise and the spring growth was apparent everywhere. On the paddocks there was a genuine greening up of grasses, calves and lambs were growing, trees were in blossom, flowers were showing their vibrancy and people were once again wearing brighter colours. Jenna had arranged to meet Anne at the cinema later that afternoon, after she had been to the Doctor. Yes Jenna thought as she sat in the waiting room it is not ideal when the Doctor phones you to make an appointment but there it is, and as with all things you need to deal with it. Jenna was reading a magazine when her name was called and she dutifully made her way down to the Doctor's office feeling like a child being called into the Headmaster's office as they were called in those days, where many a student treaded with dread in their hearts on the way there, and often sore hands on their way back to class, never an uplifting experience by all accounts, but then Jenna had been spared those long walks, in part because she had never been caught doing anything untoward, and in part because she was fortunate to have mixed with people at school who had not been prone to doing anything untoward either. Her thoughts were momentarily interrupted when she was motioned to have a seat outside the doctor's office, and as she sat down her thoughts returned to her earlier years, where she found herself wondering if she had been with the more adventurous children who on occasion found themselves walking to the headmasters office if that would have given her better skills in coping with Adam's betrayal, and deceit in her more recent adult years. The door to the doctor's office opened and she was asked in so she didn't have time to ponder on that too much.

"Now Jenna I've asked you to come in because I believe we have an answer."

"And with an answer you will have a tablet for that. Am I right? And you know how I love to take tablets."

"Yes I do, so you will be delighted to know that you can now come off the one tablet you have been taking."

"My iron tablet?"

"Yes. For some reason your body has decided to store iron up which is totally opposite to what it was doing before, which is why I put you on iron tablets."

"Are you sure?"

"Absolutely. Bloods don't lie Jenna. No more iron tablets for you, and everything else looks fine as far as your blood work goes. You could still lose a few kilos, but apart from that keep on doing what you are doing, and if there are any changes come back and see me."

"You could have got your nurse to phone me and tell me that."

"Yes I did have that option, but then I would not have seen the pleasure on your face at not having to take the one tablet I have prescribed for you."

"Did you used to make visits to the Headmaster's office?"

"Yes I did actually he used to call me a tearaway. Why do you ask?"

"What did you learn from that?" Jenna asked.

"Resilience. I learned to be myself, and how to get up and keep going and when he arrived in my office one day he sat in that very chair,"pointing to where Jenna was sitting, and said 'the one thing I learned about you in my office was that you knew exactly what you were doing all the time. You never shied away from it. I hope that quality is still there.'"

"How extraordinary. Did you give him the jab?" Jenna asked.

"Give him the jab? It is a few years since I've heard that saying. No but I did help him to leave this world with his dignity intact. He taught me that consequences hurt, that helped me when I got older."

And on that note Jenna left his office, paid the bill, made her way to the gardens for a walk around in the sunshine and reflect on how very fortunate she was. Having admired the flowers, borders and roses for some time Jenna checked her watch and made her way to the cinema,

where she hoped Anne would be there to
meet her as arranged.

KAREN PIVOTT

CHAPTER SIXTEEN

As with all things Jenna decided there was an unpredictability which kept one on one's toes so to speak and the weather was no exception. As the days were beginning to warm up ever so slightly bringing that hope of warm sunny days, before summer's arrival they were hit with a weather bomb. Jenna had never heard that expression before, an unseasonal front, a blast of cold weather, but a weather bomb? And not until the weather bomb hit did Jenna gain a true understanding of what is was and how apt the description had fitted the event.

The paddocks behind her were lakes and had it not been for the weather service putting out a warning two days before, she may well have seen floating cows while eating breakfast. Fortunately the farmer had managed to move his cows to higher ground. So severe were the winds, the rain, and the drop in temperature that people were being advised to stay indoors until the system had passed through. A consequence of a weather bomb it seemed was no communication. Power lines were down. Telephone lines were damaged. Thankfully Jenna had a mobile phone but network issues were at play there as well.

Against the advice given at the start of the event Jenna donned her hat, raincoat and gloves and made her way over to Anne's to make sure she was all right. A very frightened looking Anne answered her back door to a very wet and bedraggled Jenna.

"Are you mad Jenna?" Anne said and then threw her arms around her "Thank you for coming I am quite beside myself." Anne finished and then extricating herself from Jenna helped her get out of her wet coat hanging the coat and the hat on the coat hooks by her back door.

"You're very welcome. I thought what is the point of me sitting this out over there alone, when we could be sitting through it together? I was also thinking it was a good job we had our trees attended to by"

"Mr. Morris." Anne said finishing the sentence for Jenna. "Yes indeed, he and his team will be very busy I would imagine. Tea, coffee, something stronger?"

"Given how chatty you are and quite emboldened actually, finishing my sentences, indeed Anne, I would surmise you have had the something stronger already." Jenna said giving Anne a knowing look as she smiled.

"Well I have poured a small one and taken a sip or two, but that is all and I don't think you joining me in a tipple will do you any harm at all. And for the record my emboldened tongue as you put it was driven by sheer relief that I have been rescued."

"Rescued from what? Your property is undamaged, your gardens are good and you look perfectly fine."

"On the outside I look perfectly fine Jenna but unfortunately on the inside it is quite different. It is the sound more than anything. It has brought back some rather painful memories. Memories I thought would never see the light of day again. And there it is, the fear of loss careening to the surface. I was feeling quite sick and very shaky just like when I was on the side of the river."

"The side of the river?"

"Sit down and I will bring your drink over to you and I will tell you all about it. If you don't mind that is."

"Do you think it will help you or make it worse?" Jenna asked seeing that Anne was actually quite pale and still shaking.

"Only one way to find out isn't there?" Anne said before sitting herself and beginning her recollection of a very sad time indeed. "My brothers Andy and Bevan were at the river fishing for Trout. Andy was eleven and Bevan was fourteen. Mum was listening to the radio and heard the weather forecast that there was a front

coming in, 'the Met service advises stock
be moved to higher ground before evening"
the announcer had said, and it was so
very stern and foreboding the
announcement that Mum told me to go to
the river and tell the boys to come home.
Now the river was a good fifteen minute
walk from where we lived, and as I set off I
remember looking at the sky which was
already turning dark Grey and the cloud
cover was heavy. I was twelve and I got
this feeling that I had to make haste.

Normally I would have ambled my
way along probably taking twenty five
minutes to get there. Anyway when I got
to the river my brothers were nowhere to
be seen so I started calling them. I walked
up and down the river bank and then I
heard my brother Bevan calling out help,
help. I ran towards his voice and when I
got there I could see that Andy was caught
under a tree stump and Bevan was trying
to get him free.

Drops of rain started falling and the
wind got up and Bevan told me to stay
with Andy while he went to get a thick
branch that he could use as leverage to
get Andy free. Andy was shivering from the
cold, and now the rain was getting heavier,

and the wind was getting up, and there I was with Andy talking to him trying to keep him awake and it seemed to take forever for Bevan to come back, and then finally I heard a dragging sound, and there was Bevan with a large branch.

Bevan jumped into the river and got me to push the branch under where Andy was. Bevan dove under the water and placed the branch right under the tree stump. No matter how hard he tried the tree stump wasn't budging, and now the water was beginning to rise and was moving swiftly. I decided to go and get help. I had thought that by now Mum at least would be coming to look for us because we should have been home by then.

I ran along the river bank and out onto the road and saw Mum and two neighbours in the old farm truck. I was waving at them to stop and I explained what had happened. Everyone made their way to the boys and on the way I remember thinking thank goodness I went to the road to show them where to go. Andy will be fine now. What I remember next is seeing the men jumping into the river and pulling Bevan out. Mum covering her face and collapsing on the grass holding Bevan, and the rain pouring over the scene, the wind howling with the river raging so loudly you couldn't hear what people were saying. Then I saw the two men pull a very limp Andy out of the water. He never drew breath again." Anne said with tear sliding down her cheek.

"Oh Anne how dreadful."
"I remember thinking at the time this is my fault. I should have run back and got Mum sooner, instead of staying with Andy. I mean Andy was stuck he wasn't going anywhere, but then a part of me could see the river rising and I wanted to be there if the tree moved with the force of the river, but in the end nothing and no one could save Andy."

"So how did your neighbours get him out?"

"Well therein lies the irony Jenna." Anne said composing herself. "The force of the water cascading along the river dislodged the tree as I had hoped it would. Unfortunately that happened too late for Andy. I actually lost two brothers that day Jenna. Bevan was holding Andy when he passed from this world and a big piece of Bevan went away that day too. Bevan was never the same after that. To be fair no one was. Mum and dad carried on but the light had gone from our family. Bevan left home at fifteen and went away up North to work with the Forestry Department and he was killed eighteen months later. A very sad time. Dad followed shortly after that, heart attack and Mum, well poor mum just seemed numb for years.

When I married her words to me were "I can give you a nice wedding Anne, but the marriage is up to you and Graham. The more present you are both in it, the better it will be." I remember thinking what an odd thing for a mother of the bride to say. It made sense years later when Graham started drinking to excess of course, but I often wonder if she regretted staying after Andy died. We had been married four years when Mum collapsed on the way home from work one afternoon. Stroke. I never had the opportunity to say goodbye to her either. That's the thing about death. The finality of it and the unpredictable nature of its arrival."

"Well by the sounds of it the weather bomb as they are calling it hasn't finished visiting us yet, may I suggest a game of cards or Monopoly perhaps?"

"You may but as the lights are on over the road I think perhaps we may be in luck with a DVD instead, I had treated myself this afternoon and was going to invite you over tomorrow evening to watch it with me, but now is as good a time as any." Anne said rising to turn on the TV and put the DVD disc into the player. "Yes she said we have picture and sound. What a blessing."

And Jenna could see that for Anne it was indeed a blessing, she could turn the volume up and drown out the noise of the storm. Drowning out her childhood memories though would be another matter entirely Jenna thought, but Jenna did know someone who she thought may be able to help Anne with those. She would talk to Anne about that another time and if Anne was willing Jenna decided to help with it as well.

Having pushed pause on the DVD player Anne said "How about we have a light supper and coffee while we watch this."

"Sounds great what can I do to help?"

"You set the trays and I will get the food, and make the coffee. We have power we may as well make the best of it while it is here."

"Maybe top up the thermos in case we lose it again?" Jenna asked.

"Yes absolutely." Anne said and set about slicing cheese, cutting up the French bread loaf clearly intended for tomorrow's lunch, taking sliced meat and pickles from the fridge to add to the small platter, and a dollop of butter on a small glass plate with two knives. Anne walked over to the small table which usually resided on the wall and sat that between their two armchairs, and made the coffee, while Jenna took the trays over to the armchairs, and got some serviettes which she placed next to the platter.

Jenna sat down and placed her tray on her lap and took the cup of coffee from Anne saying, "I think I will start with the coffee and when that is empty I will start on the platter."

"You can do things in whatever order you like, but you could put the coffee on the table and start with the food. I intend to start with the food." Anne said as she put two coasters on the table, put her coffee on one, picked up her tray and sat down." Before we do anything though Jenna I will say grace if you don't mind."

"I don't mind at all. We have a lot to be thankful for Anne."

"Yes Jenna we do." Anne said as they bowed their heads.

A soon as Anne said amen Jenna added "and we should have given thanks for attending to our trees when I had that incident earlier in the year. Just imagine Anne how much damage they could have done in this storm."

"Do you know I had completely forgotten about that? What an unintended blessing that has turned out to be." Anne said.

"Fortuitous sums it up nicely. This cheese Anne delicious."

"We are all allowed treats Jenna. Enjoy."

"Thank you Anne for sharing your treats with me."

"Least I can do. Thank you Jenna for coming over. I was really beside myself." Anne replied as she pushed play and settled back in her armchair to enjoy the movie.

CHAPTER SEVENTEEN

With the storm having passed and the clean up well in hand the town was almost back to normal and the resilience of people never ceased to surprise Jenna. Yes it was pretty much life as normal to the passers-by, but then it never really is life as normal for people on a daily basis is it? Something will always be happening to, or people will always be affected by something or someone, and it was on this random thought that Jenna received a phone call she never expected to get. It was the Publishing House and the new receptionist Alison Peterson was the one making the call.

"Mrs Mitchell it is Alison Peterson calling from…." Jenna was trying to think why the receptionist was calling nothing was due to go to the Publishing House and Jenna had made it quite clear to Tania that she would not be submitting her current piece of writing until late November and so being Jenna she interrupted the receptionist mid-sentence to clarify her position by saying.

"I'm sorry Alison I am a little confused. I have told Tania that my next piece of work won't be ready until late November."

"Oh Mrs. Mitchell I am not phoning about that. I am over stepping the mark I think but I thought you should know. I mean you and Tania have quite the history everyone says so, in fact when this happened it was like who is going to tell Mrs. Mitchell."

"Yes I see, tell Mrs. Mitchell what exactly Alison?"

"Tania's husband Baz has been involved in a very serious Biking accident on his way to work. Tania is at the hospital now."

"Which hospital?" Jenna asked and made her way there as soon as she put down the phone.

On her arrival she was directed to where Tania was waiting and Jenna saw just how grave the situation was.

"Jenna how did you now?"

"You forget Tania what a great caring Boss you are, and I am not about to drop anyone in doo doo."

"I will kiss the person who rang you." Tania said.

"In that case Alison Peterson is it? She is the person who phoned me. Now tell me where are we at?"

"Not anywhere I thought I would be at all." Said Tania mopping up her tears.

"Well once we do know where things stand we can make a plan. I am prepared to wait with you if that helps? If not I am just as happy to leave you in peace."

"You Jenna Mitchell had better get yourself comfortable we could be in for a long night." Tania said as Jenna squeezed her hand in support and they made their way to the chairs.

As it turned out it was long night which extended well into the next day, but twenty four hours after the accident a very banged up, well plastered, stitched and bruised Sebastian was declared stable, and in an induced coma to allow his brain some healing time.

Tania made her way home to their children and thanked Jenna for her support and Jenna made her way to a local cafe to collect herself before she drove home, and as she was sitting at the table waiting for her Flat White and Ham and Cheese Croissant to arrive she took a deep breath bowed her head and uttered words of thanks not caring there were other people around who could hear her. "Thank you for the surgeons and medical staff who have worked tirelessly and skilfully on Sebastian, and for his full and speedy recovery."

"Excuse me are you all right?" Suz asked Jenna as she put her food and coffee down on the table.

"Oh yes it has just been a night. Thank you Suz for asking." Jenna said reading her name badge, as she felt the wetness on her cheeks that Suz had obviously seen.

Having eaten her meal Jenna went home and got on with her day determining an early night would be in order.

Early that evening Tania phoned Jenna with an update, and Tania explained that Baz would be laid up for some time. He was still in the induced coma and his recovery would be quite involved, but a full recovery in time was expected.

"I'm a publisher and you are the words smith and honestly Jenna what does any of that mean? Involved. Involved. Involving what? Who? Where? These are details one should be given." Tania said her exasperation transcending the phone line.

"Perhaps it's their way of saying he is out of the woods but not ready to walk the road to home yet? Take a breath Tania and be thankful he is still with you all. I am. Without putting too fine a point on it, the prognosis this time last night was not looking very hopeful at all."

"Oh Jenna you are right. What am I thinking? What do I care about the what? Who? Or the where? My Sebastian is still here and that is all that matters."

And with that the phone line went dead. It was at that moment that Jenna realised the gravity of the situation had actually only just hit Tania. In all the years Jenna had known Tania she had literally heard her use his full name only twice before, and that was when she was talking about the birth of their children. "Full names are for significant events in one's life the rest of the time he is Baz. He prefers Baz you see, but I think Sebastian is a lovely name. We had a Golden Retriever called Sebastian when I was growing up. I remember that coming up on our first date, and he said right there and then I prefer to be called Baz."

Jenna had smiled at this "No wonder he goes by Baz who would want to be mistaken for a Golden Retriever?"

"Do you know I never thought of that?" Tania had said looking at Jenna, and they both laughed only to be interrupted by the man himself "What are you two laughing at?"

"It is more a case of what are the two of us laughing about, and it is your name Sebastian who now goes by Baz." Jenna said.

"Well I would never have been loved the same as the original now would I?" Baz said with a wink.

The following morning Jenna popped over to see Anne who had received a letter from Dot their neighbour who was living away and it was great to hear all her news.

"Do you know Anne when people leave a place there really is a void isn't there? New people come in of course and add their vibrancy or presence but it's not the same."

"I daresay it's not the same for them either Jenna. You know it can take a while for some people to settle in and feel comfortable, accepted, no at home in their new environment and I think we forget that." Anne said.

"I suppose you have a point. I mean when I shifted here with Adam, we had our son and his family here, but then we were leaving a fractured situation at the time in the place we were, and well it was more of an escape rather than a new start so it was going to be different and then fate intervened and the first twelve months is a still a bit of a blur."

"As Dot says it has been a huge change for her but she is loving it and meeting loads of new people. You know Jenna I can't quite put Dot and that content together. Dot and loads of people. I mean she was nearly always out and about on her own here even when she was married.”

“New lease on life it sounds like and good for her. I am so pleased she is happy there. Have you met the new neighbour in her place?” Jenna asked.

“No. I don’t think anyone has actually shifted in yet. I know Mr Lawn Master arrives every fortnight to keep the grounds ship shape but that’s it really. Are you getting excited about your trip? Christmas is on its way to a home near you was the advertisement in one of our local shops this morning.”

“Christmas comes but once a year my father used to say, and for the life of me I can’t understand why we have to rush its arrival.” Jenna told Anne.

“Am I excited?” Jenna said looking thoughtful before she answered “I am looking forward to spending time with Jason and Eden, the Texas leg, to be honest the jury is out on that one but I am up for a challenge and more than happy to receive pleasant surprises as you know.”

“Who are you kidding Jenna Mitchell you make the best of every situation you find yourself in that is why you are so successful.” Anne said.

"Thank you but how does one measure success? I thought we could drop off a Christmas basket of goodies for the staff at the hospice shop. They do a great job there fund raising so that those who are dealing with the end times can do so with dignity and support. Do you know how many volunteers work there?"

"Unsurprisingly no, but there is a phone book handy so I will ring to see who's in charge and speak to them shall I?"

"Oh thank you Anne that would be so kind. Can you let me know later so I can get a few things together, and when it gets to the putting together stage I will phone you?"

"How long do you think this putting together project is going to take?" Anne asked.

"Just a few hours, we could do it one evening or one afternoon, or even one morning whatever suits you best."

"I will have to consult with my diary I am quite in demand this year. I will let you know." Anne said walking over to the phone book and as Jenna left she wasn't quite sure whether Anne was really quite in demand or being facetious, what Jenna did know was that Anne would be available and they would have a very relaxed time putting the packs together.

Literally within the hour Anne had phoned Jenna with the information that was required right down to where the packs could be left for the volunteers to pick up. Anne was quite surprised by how many volunteers were involved and thought this might cause Jenna to modify her project and expressed that in her call "There are thirty volunteers all up who have helped this year some more than others. There are fifteen core helpers if you want to concentrate on them."

"Absolutely not I think we will do 40 packs there will be the odd family in need they know of as well."

"Jenna isn't this going to be expensive for you?"

"Some people give money, some people give time, some give goods, and they never stop to think how expensive it is, they just do it don't they? I like to give appreciation for those who serve and the feel good factor far out ways the cost. I will get the items and can you consult with your diary to let me know which day next week will suit you, and the time please."

"Friday morning and I will make myself available all day." Anne said as she put the phone down and she knew right then that the anonymous Santa for the Volunteer Fire Brigade last year was Jenna and there had been other recipients over the last few years as well.

As Anne was pondering on that Jenna was answering her phone again "Jenna its Jean I am just ringing to see how things are with you?"

"I am just busy enough. And how are you?"

"I am great. I am sitting outside with a cup of coffee and enjoying our landscaped area, the plants have come on now and it very peaceful indeed. I just wanted you to know that shifting here was the right decision for me even though I miss you. I am looking forward to us catching up next year and I was wondering if you were still doing your appreciation packs this year?"

"Yes I am, and I am roping Anne in to help me with them."

"Who is the lucky service group this year may I ask?"

"Well I thought Hospice this year Jean in memory of Roy. He certainly appreciated all they did for him."

"Oh Jenna that is lovely. Have you started packing for your trip yet?"

"No I haven't, but perhaps I should start thinking about that the weeks tend to slip away rather quickly at this end of the year. Now tell me how are the Fellowes? Cyril and Joy looking forward to their break away together I am sure." And in no time at all an hour had passed and neither of them had noticed it.

CHAPTER EIGHTEEN

Jenna was relishing getting the items and the baskets for her appreciation project. Every day she woke with a joyful heart and she got through her lists of chores. Jenna had ordered some gift boxes on-line and was very pleased when they arrived at her front door.

They were going to be just big enough which would make the packing of them much easier. Jenna had purchased forty packets of everything small Christmas Cakes, mince tarts, nuts and raisins, festive serviettes, small boxes of chocolates, pretzels, and popcorn, and of course a card to say thank you for each box.

Jenna was happy with the contents and was counting down the days to putting them all together with Anne and then dropping them off. Yes Jenna smiled as she put the boxes with the goods in the spare bedroom, this felt good and she said as much to the Hat as she made her way back to her Kitchen where she had left the phone.

It was movie night and Jenna had forgotten to book a table for her and Anne which normally would not have been a problem, but on this occasion it was, so Jenna decided they would have Roast Hut meals for dinner and phoned Anne to let her know there was a change in plan and apologise for her slackness.

"You slack? Jenna give me a break. Roast Hut is fine. I will pick you up at two o'clock our movie starts at two forty five, unless you want to do something first?" Anne asked.

"Two o'clock sounds great to me I will be ready. See you then." Jenna said and although it was only eleven o'clock Jenna decided to sit and put her feet up for a bit, and that bit turned out to be over two hours. Jenna woke up to the sound of the phone ringing, and as she was trying to get the phone off the occasional table next to her she was not quite believing that she had actually fallen asleep, "Hello" she said as looked over at the clock, and saw that the clock was telling her it was after one o'clock.

"Is that you Jenna? It is Tania. Just a quick call to let you know your royalty payment is in your account, and it is bigger than what you normally receive, and no it is not a mistake."

"Pardon? What books?"

"You will see. And the award dinner next Friday night. All that is in the email. Must dash have an appointment with the Physiotherapist they are setting up the treatment plan for Baz, oh and Jenna please spend some of the money on you. You have earned it after all, and just so you know I am thrilled for you. This Jenna Mitchell is what success in monetary terms looks like when you have a best seller. Enjoy Jenna talk soon."

Jenna sat quite stunned. Tania never phoned about royalty payments they just arrived in her account and Jenna let them sit there to fund her small philanthropic endeavours. The irony being that Jenna started writing to supplement income when her children were small, and now she had more than she needed every day. She often thought why am I getting a bigger amount of money now? Jenna was bemused by this and couldn't understand why her book sales had suddenly increased so substantially. Another look at the clock stopped that thought process. "I must get moving Anne will be here soon." Jenna said to the room as she vocalized her next action and with that she got up and headed passed the hat hanging on the wall in the hallway and down to her room where she changed into a dress and her good shoes. Smiling to herself she wondered if she put on a large hat to finish the look but as she did actually own a large hat that was never going to happen. She did however find a rather smart jacket to complete the outfit and checked her look in the bedroom mirror. "Is this how a best-selling author presents oneself to the world?" she asked the mirror and smiled.

Anne was on time which was no surprise. Anne had been on time for everything after three months of widowhood had passed, and continued to be on time, never late, never early, Jenna on the other hand was usually early, often on time and invariably late on occasion. Oh yes Jenna thought as she climbed into her car, you rather do like to mix things up it keeps people on their toes. Pity you didn't do that when you were married to Adam.

"You look quite lost in thought Jenna?" Anne commented as Jenna was putting her seatbelt on.

"Random thoughts. Really Anne I don't know where they come from."

"I meant to ask you earlier have you heard from Tania? How is Baz doing?"

"Well Anne as a matter of fact I have just got off the phone with her, and they have a meeting with the Hospital Physiotherapist today for Baz's treatment plan, so I would say things are progressing steadily."

"He is one lucky man if you ask me." Anne said.

"I think you will find it is Tania who is feeling lucky right now. Baz on the other hand is still feeling very pained." Jenna said as they made their way to find parking with Jenna completely omitting to mention the fact that her book sales had soared.

The following morning Jenna received a phone call from her bank "Good morning may I speak with Jenna Mitchell please?"

"You are speaking with Jenna."

"It is Brad Rowe here from the Auckland Savings Bank I was just wondering if you were expecting a large deposit in your account today?"

"Well I am pleased that the deposit I was told to expect has obviously arrived, but I wasn't given the figure of it over the phone, and to be honest I haven't had time to check my emails or bank account as yet."

"Can you tell me where you were expecting this deposit to come from?"

"Well my publisher of course. They do send through deposits regularly. Is there a problem?"

"I don't believe so it is just that when there is an anomaly we like to make sure that all is in order. Would you like to come in and have a chat with me Mrs.

Mitchell? We could discuss how to best put this money to work for you.”

“Really? What’s wrong with it just sitting there for a bit? You know Brad I do wonder sometimes if the bank knows who owns the money that is going into accounts.   I mean what if I want to buy a car or something with it in a few days. You know just spend it.” Jenna said quite crossly.

“I would be very pleased for you Mrs. Mitchell however I will be happy to help you park and earn the balance after that?” Brad asked.

“I beg your pardon.” Jenna said.

“We are talking a sizable deposit.”

“I am confused Brad. I mean I get deposits into my account as I said regularly and no one from the bank has ever phoned me before, well that’s not quite true, when the insurance monies went in I got a call but that was.”

“It is the banks policy to phone the customer if deposits over a certain amount are made.”

“Well I am quite busy this afternoon do you have a spot this morning?”

“Yes I do shall we say eleven o’clock?”

"Do you have an earlier time?" Jenna asked.

"Nine thirty?"

"Nine thirty, yes I can be there at nine thirty. See you then." Jenna said putting the phone down, glancing at the clock and making her way to the kitchen to collect her car keys. Twenty minutes would be enough time to get into town, find parking and meet this Brad Rowe at the bank.

On her arrival at the bank Brad was there to meet her and direct her to his office.

"Nice to meet you Mrs. Mitchell now as I was saying on the phone this meeting is to ascertain where best we can place your money to earn you more money from it."

"Yes, yes and if you want me to do any business with you at all you had better start calling me Jenna."

"Jenna. Yes I see. Have you had a chance to look at your account yet?

"No. I got busy getting here to you." Jenna said "And I must say it feels rather odd. It's just my royalties as I said on the phone, and my Publisher rang to say it was more than usual, but I really haven't

had time to give it any thought at all. I
would have checked it later today but I am
here now so.”

"Yes well I am pulling up your
details now and as you can see.”

"Oh my” said Jenna “I can certainly
see.”

"Any thoughts on how you would
like us to manage it for you in the short,
medium, or long term”

"I think some in each of those” said
Jenna and I will put some across into my
everyday account so I can load some onto
my travel card. I am going overseas
shortly.” Jenna said still trying to process
the figure she had just seen.

"I was thinking a more long term
plan. We have”

"Brad I have just said what I want
done with my money. You will see I have
money already committed in the longer
term with your bank and I have other
investments as well. The term longer is
relative to where one is at, at any given
moment in time. My longer is set already
and for the moment I am quite happy to
have some money available in the now,
short and medium term, to enjoy, and let’s
say a third in each so a third can go into

my everyday account for now, a third for the short term and a third for the medium term. Now Brad if this is a problem for you or your bank I am quite happy."

"Jenna it is no problem at all." Brad said trying very hard to smooth the feathers he had obviously ruffled.

"Good I will sign some paperwork then, so you can transfer some around, but the everyday account amount is an early Christmas present for me." And as Jenna uttered those words she knew there would be unexpected Christmas joy for others as well, exactly who she had not yet determined, but to share joy around was the best gift of all. As Jenna returned home she estimated what the temperatures would be when she was on her trip and went through her wardrobe to start the packing process.

Walking along the hallway on her way to the kitchen to put the jug on Jenna said to the Hat "I could always buy a few items of clothing while I'm away. I don't usually I know but that doesn't mean I can't does it?" Jenna asked and with the movement of the sun reflecting through the lounge window Jenna could have sworn the hat winked his approval at her.

Later that very afternoon Jenna received a call from her financial adviser Neil Milton about an investment that was coming due, and they discussed options over the phone for that pot of money, and it occurred to Jenna that perhaps she needed a more cohesive plan.

"I am away shortly for a few weeks. I will be back late January. Perhaps we could meet in February and look at things again."

"February how about the second week in February the Tuesday say nine o'clock. I remember you like to have early starts, so if that is still the case?"

"Yes I have just made a note of that on my calendar. As I won't see you before Christmas enjoy the time with your family. But then again your family is growing up now so I daresay the mates and or girlfriends will be changing things up a bit." Jenna suggested.

"I don't know how you remember those details, and yes you are right. Actually it will be the first Christmas we have been relegated to a Christmas evening get together. Feels a bit odd to be honest."

"All things experienced for the first time either feel odd, great or awful, but what never changes is the fact that you are dealing with something different, and differences Neil keep us engaged with life."

"I hadn't thought of it quite like that. Look forward to seeing you in February. As always Jenna a real pleasure to talk with you." Neil said ending their conversation.

It should be a pleasure Jenna thought I was one of the few clients who stayed loyal to you and your company through the global financial crisis, but that was another story that for many ended very badly, but fortunately for Jenna did not impact her at all, and that was due solely to Neil not throwing caution to the wind and investing in things that looked very good. Too good. As Jenna recalled at that time Neil took a lot of flak for those decisions, but as he said to Jenna on one occasion, "I have to advise you of your options, but Jenna I also need to sleep at night with a clear conscious and some of these things, they don't feel right. Now of course I can't tell you what to do."

"Thank you Neil. I think we will leave things where they are. If I don't make as much I can live with that. If I lose a lot or the lot, well at the moment I'm not sure I could manage quite so well. So we will stay the course."

Until now it had never occurred to Jenna that Neil would also have taken a financial hit by being cautious when others around him were getting higher fees and higher bonuses, but then Neil was still there, and so were a core group of his clients. Sitting down with her now freshly made coffee Jenna said to the world "There are some good people in the commercial world, who put the welfare of others before their own personal gain, we are truly blessed."

CHAPTER NINETEEN

The awards dinner had been and gone and it all went by in a blur for Jenna really. Her non-fiction book 'Living Longer' picked up best non-fiction book for the year and Tania was thrilled.

"This has brought quite a ray of sunshine in through the clouds of this year." She said giving Jenna a kiss on the cheek and sending her up to receive the award, which was something Jenna had not been expecting to do at all. Jenna only agreed to go to support Tania really and that was after she had tried twice to get out of going at all.

From Tania's point of view it was exactly the right time as Jenna's latest book the third in her non-fiction trilogy was about to hit the book stands across the country and be available to overseas customers as well.

Radio and television interviews for Jenna followed and then a few pod casts and it was not as if Jenna had lots of time to spare.

Then there were the congratulatory phone calls and emails and the busyness meant that Jenna was sitting on a plane heading to a very excited and very happy Mother and Son before she knew it. Apart from some turbulence on the way which was more an annoyance than a problem, Jenna was enjoying her flight and was thankful for the empty seat beside her.

Jenna used her flying time to reflect on the events, people and places she had been involved with or had been to, over the year and it had been a very full year indeed.

The day before she left Jenna had met up with Pam and the young members of the coffin group and Jenna dispersed presents and Christmas cheer, and said her goodbyes knowing there was a high chance that two very special people would not be alive on her return.

This was the cold harsh reality of things, and all those involved with the coffin club learned to deal with this in their journey, and they all embraced the inevitable very well.

Jenna who had been to many farewells had decided that it was time to leave Pam to train up a new person to assist her in her work so the journey for others would continue to be a positive one.

Jenna thought long and hard about what she would be doing in the coming year, and apart from her upcoming cruise she actually didn't have anything planned out, and perhaps for one year that might become the plan. More spontaneity, less structure. Jenna smiled thinking "Where is the hat when I need him?"

Settling in to watch another movie Jenna was interrupted only by the arrival of drinks, and a meal. On her arrival at the airport Jason and Eden were both waving, there were hugs, and smiles and Jenna felt a distinct drop in temperature.

"Jenna where is your coat. You did bring one?" Eden asked.

"How far is it to your place from here?" Jenna asked.

"About an hour." Jason said.

"And there is a heater in your vehicle?"

"Yes Jenna of course there is." Jason said.

"Well let's get on then. I can't wait to see where you live and get a real feel for the place."

"It is sitting on your armchair by the front door isn't it? Your coat?"

"Oh Jason you think you know me so well, but actually I thought your Mum and I could go shopping for a new coat for me, and have some girl time."

"Oh Jenna I do like the sound of that, and as it happens Jason has to go to work in the morning so that works out perfectly."

"Good save Jenna." Jason said with a smile and a wink as he put Jenna's suitcase into the boot of the car.

Unbeknown to Jason, Jenna had planned to purchase a new coat while she was away, but had thought that would happen on the second leg of her journey.

The projected temperatures where Jason and Eden live, had been much higher than her legs were feeling right now.

"We tried to get hold of you to warn you of the cold snap. Our weather is completely out of sorts this year." Eden said as they were driving along the highway.

"That seems to be the norm all around the globe at the moment." Jenna said and settled back in her seat taking in the scenery. "So much traffic Jason how do you stand it?" Jenna asked.

"Like everything Jenna you get used to it and adapt accordingly." Jason said confidently.

The drive to the apartment was quite long and Jenna found herself nodding off at one stage. It was Eden's voice that rallied her. "Jenna we thought we would have a bite to eat here."

"Oh yes, all right then. How much further is it?"

"Just around the corner a bit." Jason said.

"Perhaps we could go home first and then walk back for something to eat. I don't mind walking."

"In this weather Jenna we are not walking. You are not at home now." Eden said as Jason opened the door to a freezing blast of cold air, and Jenna mused that was the end of that conversation.

The following morning Eden and Jenna dropped Jason off at work and headed to a small local shopping complex.

"I must confess Eden I thought we would be going to a large mall." Jenna said.

"That is an option and there is a factory outlet mall not far from here as well, but I thought we could have a look here first and start the day gently." Eden informed her kindly.

"Thank you. I must say the Christmas decorations are lovely. Not too much. Everything is so big here, the scale of everything I should say, compared with home I mean." Jenna said expressively.

"Yes I know exactly what you mean and I can tell you I am still not used to it." Eden said putting her arm around her. "You know Jenna I used to be so jealous of you, the time you spent with Jason and then he said to me one day, 'Why can't you see that Mrs. Mitchell is helping me to reach my potential because she knows it is financially beyond us at the moment. Every minute I do things for her or with her I am grateful very grateful, but she is not my mum, and doesn't want to be.' You know Jenna I felt so guilty at not being able to" and Jenna interrupted before Eden could finish her sentence.

"We agreed a couple of years ago that we would not revisit this subject. I hold no animosity towards you Eden you did your very best, and you are a great mum. I am so pleased we are having this special time together, to see Jason succeeding not just hearing about it is a true blessing. Now please direct me to the shop which sells the coats."

"Just along this lane from memory." Eden said and as they entered the shop Jenna saw a coat with a matching hat, and glove set on special, in royal blue. "May I try those on please?" she asked the saleswoman.

"Certainly and we have this in red and green." She said.

"What type of green?" Jenna asked.

"Forest green I believe I can check for you." She answered and walked to the rear of the shop while Jenna with the coat, hat and gloves, went to the fitting room. The fit was very good and Eden approved of the style but they both felt the blue was just a tad too bright for Jenna. It was at this moment that the Saleswoman returned with the forest green set which Jenna tried on and they all agreed it was much better, so the Saleswoman scanned then removed the tags and Jenna left the shop proudly wearing her new coat, hat and gloves, and feeling considerably warmer than she had when she arrived.

"Do I look swish or what?" Jenna asked Eden as they walked along the cobbled pathway.

"I think you look as if you need a pair of green stockings to complete the look." Eden said with a smile.

"I do not." Jenna replied.

"I think you look lovely. Green suits you."

"Whether it suits me or not is immaterial really, I feel comfortable and I am very warm." Jenna said.

"And let's not forget you are looking swish. Is swish the female version of dapper?" Eden asked.

"Well I suppose it is. I've never really thought about it. It is a saying my mother used that her mother had used before her."

"Language the evolving tool over time, peoples and places." Eden said.

They continued their walk along the paved paths entering into shops and browsing as they went. Eden bought a few things for Christmas presents and Jenna picked up a couple of Christmas decorations to take home with her as a memento. Eden's phone rang just as they were about to enter a gift shop "Its Jason I will just take this." Eden said stepping to the side of Jenna and Jenna stepped away from the doorway.

Everything was so lovely. The Christmas decorations that were hung, the music that was playing, not too loud, quite different from a mall Jenna thought, natural light, natural temperature, just like when I was a girl Jenna thought and allowed herself a brief time of reflection, which was interrupted by Eden's voice "Jason is going to be finishing late, he sends his apologies."

"Will that mean you will have to go and get him in the dark?"

"No he has arranged to get home. What it means is that I have company tonight which is a change I can tell you."

"He works late a lot then?"

"When certain projects are on, yes. He will not be working Christmas Day though, he has blocked a few days out. He said to tell you he has spoken to David as arranged so they all know you have arrived safe and sound. As Jason has ditched us perhaps we could have a leisurely lunch. There is a family restaurant not far from here. What do you think?"

"I am rather at the mercy of your local knowledge I'm afraid, but whatever you think is best."

And without further ado the browsing continued all be it at a more subdued pace than before, and when all the shops had been perused, and the product within browsed or purchased, Eden and Jenna made their way to the family restaurant.

They arrived about one o'clock and seemed to be between groups of diners. Those who were leaving, those who were arriving such as themselves, and a couple of tables where the dining appeared to be in full swing. There was a group in particular rather large in number who were definitely in the middle of something. An early Christmas celebration perhaps or maybe a birthday or anniversary. Everyone at the table was dressed in what Jenna's grandmother would have described as 'in their finery', some were laughing, and some of them were speaking very loudly. Jenna's observation was interrupted by the waitress who said "If you would follow me."

Once Jenna and Eden were seated, the waitress went to get some menus. A drinks person came to take their order and Jenna was admiring the Christmas decorations, when they were both alerted to the loud voices becoming more raised.

Eden had a look of absolute horror on her face, and Jenna turned to see what had alarmed her. The elderly woman in the large group was on her feet, pointing a gun at some of the people at the table and shouting "You have stolen from me long enough. Take, take, take, well, we'll see about that."

There were frantic scenes all around. At the table itself. At the table to the right of that one, the waitress was on the phone, and had dropped to the floor taking cover under a table and Jenna was quite incredulous as to the scene unfolding before her. Eden was calling her name "Jenna get on the floor."

Jenna who was not as sprightly these days found that to be a curious request, but never the less she complied, not as gracefully as she would have liked, but complied she did, and managed to crawl to the same side of the table as Eden.

"Well so much for a leisurely lunch." Jenna said softly.

The look on Eden's face said it all. There would be no lunch leisurely or otherwise today.

Sirens could be heard in the distance and Jenna reached forward to get her handbag from the seat.

"What are you doing?" Eden asked her.

"Getting my bag out of sight and I suggest you do the same." Jenna said.

What seemed like forever but was actually only four hours finally came to an end, when the lady dropped her gun to the floor dissolving into tears, and there were

police officers coming in from multiple
entry points.

Everyone was asked to stay put, and
everyone was questioned and when a
middle aged officer came to talk with Eden
and Jenna, Jenna asked "Could you
please have the music turned down or off,
if I hear Silver Bells one more time I think
I will explode."

"Certainly ma'am." He said and like
magic the restaurant was music free.

Once the interviews were done
people were free to leave, and Jenna found
herself quite shaken by the whole event as
did Eden.

"Will you be all right to drive Eden
or would you like to take a few moments?"

"Yes I think that is a good idea. We
will just sit here for a few moments."
Eden said unlocking the car.

CHAPTER TWENTY

When Jason came home rather late that evening it was to find both Jenna and Eden still up, drinking mugs of hot chocolate.

"I thought you two would have been well and truly asleep by now." He said.

"I'm afraid we are both finding sleep an elusive companion this evening." Jenna told him.

"Too much shopping?" Jason asked with a smile. "We heard on the radio there was an incident at that family restaurant we go to Mum.”

"Do you know Jason now that you are home I think I will try my pillow again. Have you finished your chocolate Jenna?”

"Yes I have." Jenna said handing her mug to Eden. "I think I will turn in as well. Will you be at work tomorrow Jason?”

"No. I am having tomorrow off and we have lots to talk about. I thought we could go out for lunch as that was interrupted today. What do you think?”

Eden and Jenna looked at each other and Eden said "We will talk about that in the morning. Goodnight Jason.”

The following morning while they were having breakfast the news covered the event of the previous day informing the listeners that no shots were fired and a peaceful surrender was managed by the Police department. There was no risk to public safety.

"They wouldn't have said that if they were actually there." Eden said.

"What do you mean if they were actually there?” Jason asked.

"Inside the restaurant." Eden informed him.

"That Jason is where we went for lunch, but we didn't get to eat anything. It was all very intense, and then very long, and from what I could surmise between Silver Bells and the shouting, the lady at the centre of the whole thing just needed to be heard and have things taken from her returned or money paid back. It was all rather surreal."

"Such a quiet part of the city."

"Wasn't so quiet yesterday Jason. But on the bright side Jenna did get her coat."

"With matching hat and gloves." Jenna added.

"Well might I suggest we go for a drive and show Jenna our neck of the woods in daylight?" Jason offered up.

"That would be lovely" Jenna said and went to get her coat, hat, gloves and handbag. On her return to the dining area where Eden and Jason were ready and waiting for her she asked "Would you be able to take me to a bag shop I think I need a green or green and black bag to finish the look."

"We can only try." Jason said with a smile and Jenna wondered if he disapproved of the colour choice she had made.

Some while later as they were nearing an outlet mall Jason said "You know I think green looks good on you. Why haven't I seen you wear it before?"

"I was never encouraged to wear colour. It has taken me years, but in truth if you had seen the blue, and I have a red jacket at home, so I stepped forward boldly and put this on."

"We all agreed she looked fab!" Eden said.

"Well let's see if fab can be completed with a matching handbag." Jason said pulling into a parking space.

Not only did Jenna find a matching bag, the bag came as a set of many bags so she purchased the set. The day went by very quickly. There were people everywhere, but that was relative to the space around them. Lots of people, lots of space, lots of busyness, lots of noise, and decorations and yes Silver Bells was joined by Jingle Bells on a rotation.

After a full day which included a quick lunch, more browsing and sightseeing, followed by a leisurely dinner, before making their way home.

"Thank you both so much. Would you be offended if I went to bed? I feel quite done in." Jenna asked.

"I won't be far behind you" Eden said.

Once Jenna had retired Jason asked "Are you all right Mum?"

"Yes, and before you ask so is Jenna. You know she was so practical, pulled her handbag off the seat, told me to do the same. The Officer who interviewed us commented on that. Apparently people scan the seats to see how many people are there. That didn't happen in our case, but how would Jenna know something like that?" Eden asked.

"One thing I know about Jenna is there is an awful lot of information in that head of hers, and it pops out on a regular basis. Good night mum see you in the morning."

The following two days saw Jason back at work and Eden and Jenna shopping for last minute Christmas things, and on Christmas Eve they had a light meal with egg nog before retiring.

And so it was when they rose the following morning Christmas Day had arrived, and so it seemed had Santa.

There were presents galore under the tree, including the one's Jenna had brought over for Eden and Jason, and a sense of anticipation in the air that Jenna hadn't felt in years.

"Merry Christmas Jenna. Mum is making waffles. I have waited for this day for eight years. Me spoiling you on a Christmas Day, and before you protest I want to make it clear that nothing is going to stop me. I can show you my appreciation finally and you must allow me to do that Jenna."

"I can see that to try and stop you would be a frivolous endeavour, but there is no need. Your success is payment enough. I believed in you yes, but you Jason Gibb have delivered big time."

"Yes he has" said Eden "breakfast is ready."

And as Jenna sat down to the breakfast feast she felt very appreciated indeed.

The day interspersed with phone calls from all the family from their places of residence, and a good long walk, not forgetting the present giving which took quite some time filled the day in perfectly, and as Christmas day came to a close with

a mug of Irish coffee, Jenna thanked Eden
and Jason from the bottom of her heart.
"The highlight for me has been the
beautiful ring you gave your mum. Thank
you Jason for arranging my Christmas
this year I have loved every minute of it."
Jenna said.

"And I have loved doing it for you,
and thank you for our precious reminders
of home. You know it doesn't matter how
busy you get there are days you just want
the familiar of home around you. I will be
kept very busy in my new job, and mum
has a new job to start in the New Year as
well."

"Eden why didn't you say anything?"
Jenna asked.

"Because I just found out last night
and we wanted this Christmas to be about
you. You have brought many blessings to
this family Jenna, and having the photos
of home and the mementos, very
thoughtful. Jenna are you sure you don't
want to go to Vincent's?"

"Oh yes that. We will talk about
those developments tomorrow but no.
There is a firm plan in place for them next
Christmas. I will explain all that in the

morning." And on that note Jenna took her leave.

The days seemed to pass by in a flash, and the New Year was welcomed in by the three of them in a rather muted fashion, but a very enjoyable one, and just a few days later Jenna found herself packing her suitcase, and the backpack that had been included in her handbag set, as well as the large handbag, so that all her things could fit onto the plane for the next leg of her trip, and when they were at the terminal with Jenna's baggage checked in tears were flowing, with smiles and hugs. By the time Jenna took her seat she felt quite exhausted, and somewhat apprehensive. Jason had included trips and stay overs and lots of sightseeing Jenna's head was still reeling from it all. Take a breath Jenna thought you will be home with the Hat for company soon enough. Just one more leg of the trip to go.

As the plane landed and Jenna made her way to the baggage carousel, Jenna was feeling quite rested, and having collected her suitcase she made her way with all the other passengers to the arrivals lounge to a smiling Penelope.

"Oh Jenna we are just so thrilled that you are here. Let me take your suitcase, and your bags. How on earth did you get on the plane with all those? I have parked quite close. Now we are meeting Duane on the way home. He has a surprise for you, and before you say anything it is justly deserved." Penelope was saying as she walked with purpose.

Jenna following behind was feeling somewhat confused, as if something was going on without her knowledge and it was culminating in a very uneasy feeling. Once in the car, they vacated the parking building and were on the busy wide streets of the city, and at a set of lights Penelope turned left and drove into a large car park. Pulling into a reserved space Penelope turned to Jenna and said "We are meeting Duane here. Follow me."

Which Jenna did wondering what she had let herself in for and it wasn't long before she heard Duane's familiar booming voice announcing something, and as she got closer she heard her name and clapping, and as she followed Penelope up some stairs she was met with a huge hug from Duane followed by the words "Straight off the plane in the flesh our award winning Jenna Mitchell ladies and gentlemen." Followed by more applause.

Jenna quite taken aback found herself looking out at a sea of people, with Duane and Penelope flanking her, and a microphone in front of her.

"Now Jenna we know this is something new for you, but all these people have come out to say thank you for your books, which have helped them and their loved ones immensely, and if you could just say a few words." Duane said, and Jenna began by thanking everyone for coming and expressed her genuine surprise at how the day had not gone at all as she had expected it would. The audience were great and laughed along with her.

There had been speakers from different organizations who had gone before her, which complimented her subject matter, and Jenna's timely arrival had fitted perfectly with the panel discussion that was about to take place that Jenna took part in, and then the stage was cleared and Jenna was shown to a table where there were rows of books including her new release, and several pens and Duane pulled a chair out for her as customers lined up to get a signed copy of the books there, and those they had brought with them, and over three hours later Jenna was being driven to their home and quite in awe of what had just happened.

"I am so proud of you Jenna. Given that Tania only told you about this three weeks ago I think you handled it extremely well. What do you think honey? A natural or what? And you were worried."

"Tania. Yes well I am glad someone other than you and the thousands of people in there knew about it, because I can assure you Tania said nothing to me about it." Jenna said quite curtly and then she remembered Baz and his accident, and recovery and gave Tania a pass, she must have forgotten. She had given Jenna the heads up about the royalty payment which now made perfect sense and Jenna was wondering what the next one would look like.

Penelope and Duane were exchanging confused looks between them before Penelope said "You really didn't know?"

"I really didn't know, and maybe that was for the best because I would have refused. After all that sort of event is for star Authors and I am hardly in that category." Jenna said trying to gain some control over the situation.

"Well Jenna I am pleased to update you on your current status. You are a best-selling author in your country and here in our State, and I have arranged a few more intimate gatherings while you are here. Nothing quite as large as the one you have just attended, but there are groups of people who want to meet you and thank you. When we get home perhaps you would like to phone Tania and let her know how it went."

"After you have spoken with her first I think would be more appropriate. Now can you tell me please how this all came about?"

"Happy to do so." Duane said and once he started there was no stopping him, and as the conversation transpired it became apparent that it was Penelope who had set the ball rolling so to speak several months before when she asked if anyone had read the books by Jenna Mitchell on how to cope with the death of a loved one at the local Stroke Club, and people wanted to know where they could get the books so Duane contacted Tania who arranged to ship the books over and it had grown from there to other groups as well, and copies were donated to Hospice patients and their families and it kept on growing.

"So Jenna what do you say to that?" Duane asked.

"I am pleased my words are helping people." Jenna replied "And I would have been more pleased if I had had a heads up so my words today had been more considered and myself more prepared."

"Honestly Jenna unprepared or not you were the best speaker on that stage, and I mean that. Power point presentations are a great tool, but people need to be able to connect with their audience. You Jenna nailed that completely." Duane said with a sincerity that surprised both of the women in the car.

CHAPTER TWENTY ONE

On their arrival at "The Property" Jenna was in absolute awe of the vastness of "The Property" as they called it. Not our property, or Duane's property or the family's property or Penelope's property just 'The Property' and Jenna could see an expanse before her like no other she had seen in her life before, and gingerly asked the question "Where is the stock?"

The stock is far, far, far, away on another part of 'The Property' which we will be happy to show you tomorrow, but for now I think we need to get you home, unpacked and fed. And just so you know when we rise here on 'The Property' it is early." Duane said.

As they pulled up Jenna thought they were stopping at a complex before carrying onto the house, but no a Maid and Butler appeared to greet them, and the Butler placed all of Jenna's belongings on a small trolley and followed her and the maid to her room.

"Mrs. Mitchell I am Sarah and this is Paul. If you need anything at all while you are staying with us you only have to ask. Mr. Duane and Mrs. Penelope want you to enjoy your stay with us and be very comfortable. I can unpack your things for you, or if you prefer you can unpack at your convenience. Please follow me and I will show you your room."

After quite a walk they arrived at the room Jenna would be occupying while she was staying there and Sarah said "You have your bathroom here, a covered spa pool area there, a kitchenette to make yourself a drink, which also is stocked with snacks, teas, coffees, and a selection of soda drinks. Fresh fruit will be brought to you in the mornings. Now we will leave you to rest. There is a small button here by the bed if you need assistance of any kind during the day or night."

"Thank you Sarah. I have a grand-daughter named Sarah." Jenna said.

"Really? My grandmother named me Sarah."

"I think a rest may have to come later Sarah. I need to meet up with Duane. We have a phone call to make."

"Very well if you go with Paul he will take you to Mr. Duane" and without a single sound Sarah seemed to have gone, quickly and silently.

Paul led Jenna through the house to one of the living rooms, where Duane was sitting in a very large brown leather chair.

"How long have you owned all this?" Jenna asked.

"Me? Oh Jenna you are way too kind. This my darlin's. It is all Pen's. I remember the first time I came out here. I was ushered in and told to sit by that window. I was waiting to be collected and taken to the house to see Penelope and then she skipped in, in her shorts and tee shirt, with a smacking great smile all

across her face. Quite pleased with herself
she was."

"Yes I was. My timing was perfect.
Daddy was away that day and I managed
to get a man into the house for a decent
amount of time. My Daddy scared most
men off. He was a proud man who wanted
only Mr. Perfect for his daughter, but
sadly there are no Mr. Perfects are there?
So I settled for the next best thing and
that was the best decision I have ever
made."

"Now Pen."

"Don't you now Pen me. My man came
up with a plan that was revolutionary for
these parts and made himself useful to
Daddy."

"And what was that?" Jenna asked.

"I suggested a way we could use water
that would otherwise be wasted. Water is
such a crucial resource here, well
everywhere, and when it rains here darlin'
it pours and all that water just runs off.
Now you're never going to save all of it, but
I got to thinking if we put tanks in we
could save a fair bit of it, so I got the
plumbers to come out and we trialled a
few small tanks first and then when we got

something that worked we just made it bigger is all."

"Bigger is all. Listen to you. He saved my Daddy a fortune and we married six months later."

Duane picked up the handset and made the call to Tania and while he was talking with her Jenna had walked over to a wall which was covered with photos.

"Yes this is my family. All gone now. Everyone. My brothers killed. My Mammy dropped dead when I was eight." She said pointing to each individual person. "My Daddy. It was me and my Daddy for a long time. I was a late surprise he used to say. Not a mistake but a late surprise and now I am the only one left. I often wonder what will happen to these photos when I am gone. Our family will be gone as well, as if we have never been." Penelope said quite lost in a moment of nostalgia Jenna was thinking, when Penelope began talking again "I am so pleased you came Jenna. Most people say yes and then they change their mind. I know Duane can be overbearing at times but" Jenna interrupted Penelope by saying "But nothing. If people can't take the time to get to know people properly then it is their loss if they miss out on special friendships."

"Oh Jenna what a profound thing to say." Penelope said and was interrupted by Duane's arrival.

"Yes handing you over now. It is Tania." He said handing the handset to Jenna.

"I am so sorry Jenna. I thought I had put it all in the email to you but I hadn't. You must have thought I had thrown you to the wolves."

"At least wolves hunt in packs and circle their prey first, fortunately for me I was flanked by Duane and Penelope and didn't have the chance to run anywhere, and felt somewhat protected in the thick of it."

"You Jenna Mitchell have never run from anything in all the years I have known you. Will a large bottle of wine help you to forgive me?" Tania said.

"As you know forgiveness is a process and I am seventy percent there. Two bottles of very good Pinot Gris may help with the remaining thirty percent." Jenna said adding "How's Baz?"

"Only you Jenna could ask after someone's wellbeing having been through an ordeal yourself. He's making slow, steady progress, but he wants to be completely healed already of course. Oh before I forget you have four appearances planned over the next two weeks, but Duane will fill you in on those. Perhaps if you had a speech it might help" Tania was saying as Duane had returned and took the handset from Jenna.

"Apparently I should have a speech for these appearances." Jenna said "So I can be more prepared."

"Well Duane did have a speech written for you but he left it in the truck, maybe you could use that? Or some of it?" Penelope volunteered.

"Would you?" Duane asked.

"Well I would have to read it first." Jenna said and as dinner was being prepared the three of them worked collaboratively on the speech. As they knew the audience best Jenna thought this was a good idea, and was surprised by the relevant suggestions Penelope had to offer.

At ten o'clock they all retired for the night which was a good thing because the following morning had the three of them in the Truck making their way to the Cattle

Beasts, with breakfast under their belts well before seven.

Jenna was totally in awe of the scenery and the baroness of the land.

"How do you feed your animals?" she asked as they were approaching two small hills, which Duane drove between, to reveal literally a sea of green and huge cattle beasts eating heartily.

"The storage tanks have the water piped to strategic parts of the land and we use those parts like feeding lots for the cattle."

"Quite ingenious. So where are your staff?" Jenna asked.

"They are shifting the stock from the lower plains to higher ground. We have snow forecast so they will be busy over the coming days. These cattle will be the last to be moved. They have a cook and quarters at different points across 'The Property', and there is always a Helicopter on hand." Duane said and Jenna could see that large scale farming was a complex operation.

Every day was a busy one and Duane had managed to organise things so that the appearances were back to back over two days, and included a stay in the city for them all, which enabled Jenna to visit museums and art galleries, and get a really good feel of the city as well as relax at their homestead.

Jenna's last night with them was very moving as over dinner Jenna presented them with a parting gift. She had arranged with Paul to have the box at the ready and between the main course and dessert Jenna asked him to give it to Penelope. Duane got up from his chair to watch Penelope as she opened the box which held a piece of Pounamu otherwise known as Greenstone that she had had carved for them. The paper explained what the carving represented and they were both speechless.

"Now before you say anything just know it has met all the importation requirements."

"Oh Jenna it is magnificent."

"Well I am pleased you like it. For a small thing it is quite heavy to carry around. Ah dessert." She said smiling.

"Do you normally eat dessert?" Penelope asked.

"Not normally, but I seem to have found an extra compartment for it on this trip." Jenna said with a cheeky grin.

The following morning they left even earlier than usual. Due to the weather conditions Duane had decided they would leave a day earlier than necessary to make sure Jenna would be near the airport for her scheduled flight. The trip to the city took much longer than normal as snow was falling, and the snowploughs were trying to keep the roads clear. Nevertheless they made it and had a lovely time in the city. Never had Jenna been so pleased to have purchased a coat, hat and glove set. It was well used for most of her trip.

When the following day came to say their goodbyes after the baggage had been checked in, there were hugs, tears, smiles, and a very long coffee together before Jenna was dismissed by Duane's "by your leave Jenna and safe travel my dear", which took her quite by surprise. She waved to them both with eyes that had begun to moisten, and headed through the departure gate. Sitting down as she waited for her boarding call she reflected on a trip away that had been filled with love, laughter and joy from two sets of people that weren't her family but felt as if they were, and as Jenna heard her boarding call, she rose from her seat and boarded her flight for home, knowing she would miss them and that thanks to Penelope she would be seeing Brad at the bank again on her return.

As the plane left the ground Jenna Mitchell knew she was a very blessed lady indeed. She also knew she would be spending time with the Chambers again.

This year she thought I will be travelling for pleasure not business, and found herself looking forwards not backwards.

KAREN PIVOTT

About The Author

KAREN PIVOTT is the author of Self Help, Children's and Adult Fiction books, *and is a published radio scriptwriter with HCJB Beyond the Call with Ron Cline series 2001. Radio Southland 2004 and 2005.* Published play write "Gavin's 21st." 2000 Nelson fringe art festival and literacy specialist. Karen lives in Invercargill New Zealand with her husband. Karen loves educating and inspiring people to improve their lives and the lives of all the people they connect with.

Karen has a Facebook page "It Starts With You" where she has inspirational quotes and a weekly blog of challenges and tips to enhance the lives of her readers.

https://www.amazon.com/author/karenpivott

www.ingramcontent.com/pod-product-compliance
Lightning Source LLC
Chambersburg PA
CBHW051548030726
47592CB00001B/196